"You're pregnant," he said in a stunned voice. Then his expression changed. "*Madre de Dios,* Olivia, you're having a baby!"

Olivia stared at him helplessly, a hundred reasons she should deny it coming and going in her head. But before she could voice any of them, he spoke again, this time his voice colder, harder. "*Por Dios,* when were you going to tell me this?"

Olivia lifted her shoulders. And then, realizing there was no point in trying to deny it, she said carelessly, "Why should I tell you? You're not my husband."

Anne Mather

THE RODRIGUES PREGNANCY

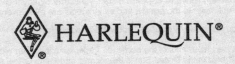

TORONTO • NEW YORK • LONDON
AMSTERDAM • PARIS • SYDNEY • HAMBURG
STOCKHOLM • ATHENS • TOKYO • MILAN • MADRID
PRAGUE • WARSAW • BUDAPEST • AUCKLAND

ISBN 0-373-12381-7

THE RODRIGUES PREGNANCY

First North American Publication 2004.

This edition published by arrangement with Harlequin Books S.A.

® and TM are trademarks of the publisher. Trademarks indicated with
® are registered in the United States Patent and Trademark Office, the
Canadian Trade Marks Office and in other countries.

Visit us at www.eHarlequin.com

Printed in U.S.A.

CHAPTER ONE

THE villa dreamed in the afternoon sunlight. Pale stone walls, blush pink tiles dripping with purple and white bougainvillea that curled over the eaves and framed the shuttered windows. There was iron grillwork circling the first floor gallery, a dark contrast to the vivid colours of the flowers. It was everything Olivia had hoped it would be and more besides.

It wasn't big. Indeed, compared to the houses she'd shared with Tony over the years, it was almost conservatively small. But that suited her. She didn't want big. She didn't want impressive. She just wanted somewhere she could call her own. Somewhere she could live unnoticed, undisturbed.

Beyond the gardens—lush lawns and rioting vegetation—the blue-green waters of the Caribbean creamed onto an almost white beach. It was delightful, it was heaven, and it was hers—for the next few months at least.

But Olivia shivered suddenly as the memory of why she was here swept over her. Tony was dead. Her husband of more than fifteen years had died as he had lived, screwing his latest mistress. And, as if that weren't enough, the police had informed her that they'd both been high on cocaine at the time.

Naturally the press had indulged in a feeding frenzy at these revelations. Antonio Mora had always been news and, even though he was dead, he'd continued to excite speculation. Particularly as his latest partner had been the wife of a local senator.

Of course that aspect of the affair had soon been hushed up, and the question of why Olivia had remained married to him for so many years had resurfaced with predictable ease. It had always been assumed that she'd overlooked his many sexual exploits because of his money. But it wasn't true. If she'd divorced Tony she'd still have been a wealthy woman. She'd signed no prenuptial agreement. A good lawyer could have probably ensured that she'd get half of everything Tony had.

No, it was Luis who had ensured that she and her husband stayed together. Luis, who had been only three when she'd come to work for Tony as the boy's nanny. And, after discovering the fiasco of their whirlwind marriage, it had been Luis she'd continued to love.

Not that Tony had been an unkind man. When they'd met for the first time, she'd been instantly attracted by his charm and good looks. What she hadn't realised was that Tony had had a different agenda. While she'd been looking for a lasting relationship, he'd been looking for a mother for his son.

He'd known she would never do anything to hurt Luis. The child had taken to her from the start and she'd let that blind her to his father's faults. Besides, after a fairly ordinary upbringing in England, she'd been flattered by Tony's interest in her. No one knew better than she did how persuasive he could be.

Tony's funeral had been a nightmare. Reporters from more than a dozen countries had been jostling for pictures of the 'grieving' widow. The fact that Olivia had found it impossible to put on a show for the media had aroused even more speculation. When she'd stood dry-eyed beside her husband's coffin Olivia hadn't realised that it would be her picture that would dominate the headlines for the following week.

Yet, she'd got over it. And she had cried, too, in her suite at the house Tony had owned in Bal Harbour. They'd been together too many years for her not to feel some emotion. And she had cared for him once before she'd learned what a liar he could be.

But, ultimately, it wasn't Tony's lies that had driven her to seek this seclusion. Her hand probed the slight swell of her stomach and her teeth dug into her lip. She was a liar, too, though there was no one now to accuse her of being a hypocrite. The guilt she had she shared with no one but herself.

And for weeks after Tony's death she hadn't allowed herself to think about what had happened the night he'd died. She'd been kept too busy sorting out his affairs to pay any attention to herself. Which was good. When her mind was busy, she could put the past behind her. She could pretend that she hadn't sacrificed her self-respect.

Avoiding Christian Rodrigues had been harder. The man who had been her husband's deputy, and with whom he had shared a common heritage, had never been easy to ignore. But he had shamed her; he had made her no better than the husband whose faithlessness she had despised. And now he was behaving as if it mattered to him what happened to her. That he had some right to say how she conducted her life from now on.

It was ludicrous. He didn't care about her. He'd proved that by seducing her that night. She couldn't bear to be around him knowing how he felt about her.

She was pretty sure he despised himself for allowing it to happen.

She knew that he'd felt sorry for her. She was too old, after all; too unglamorous to attract a man like him. Christian was like Tony. He was ambitious as well as clever. When he chose a wife, she'd have status as well as beauty.

It was when she'd discovered she was expecting Christian's baby that she'd realised she had to get away. With Luis in college in San Francisco, there was nothing to stop her from leaving Miami. San Gimeno had seemed the perfect destination, and escaping here had been easier than she'd thought.

For once, she'd appreciated the advantages that money had given her. Although much of his estate was in trust until Luis's twenty-first birthday, Tony had left her well provided for. Of the six properties he'd owned around the world, two of them—the mansion in Bal Harbour and an apartment in Miami—now belonged to Olivia. And with a trust fund that would pay her something in the region of two million dollars a year, she need never worry about security again.

Olivia had her own plans, however. As soon as— well, as soon as she returned to the States she intended to donate much of her inheritance to her favourite charities. She would keep enough for her and her baby to live on. But she had no desire for her child to know the hollow existence Luis had endured for so many years.

Nevertheless, she'd been grateful for the luxury of hiring a private jet to bring her to the island. She wanted no one to know where she was until her baby was born. She didn't want to hurt Luis, and she would miss his regular phone calls, but Christian must never know what he'd done.

One of the smaller islands in the Bahamas group, San Gimeno had been left virtually untouched by the tourist boom. There were few hotels to speak of and its economy depended on its agriculture and fishing industries. It was the perfect retreat and although she'd only been here a couple of months, she loved it already.

Leaving the veranda where she'd been sitting enjoying the view, Olivia trod across the grass to the palm-fringed dunes that edged the beach. The turf was coarse beneath her feet, but she was getting used to going barefoot. It gave her a sense of freedom and she liked it.

It was so unlike the life she'd led as the wife of one of Florida's richest men. She couldn't imagine Tony appreciating the sight of his wife wearing a simple cropped vest and denim shorts. It had been important to him to feel proud of her, and she'd got used to doing and wearing what he said.

But Tony was dead and for the first time since she was twenty-two she was her own woman. An independent being, with no one to please except herself. It was a tantalising thought. Yet she couldn't deny a shiver of—what? Anticipation? Apprehension? She wouldn't have been human if she hadn't felt some anxiety about the future.

Once again, an image of Christian Rodrigues filled her thoughts and her breath caught painfully in her throat. She had no doubt that—as she was Tony's widow—he would be there for her, too, if she needed him. But she had no intention of asking for his help. Or indeed Luis's, either.

She still hadn't decided where she was going to live after the baby was born. She might return to Florida or she might stay here. She might even go back to England. It would depend what she intended to do with the rest of her life. Whether the tentative ideas she had for earning her own living might bear any fruit.

The sun was still hot upon her shoulders, and Olivia shifted restlessly. She was used to the heat. Florida could be unbearably hot and the humidity there was much greater than it was here. Nevertheless, she didn't want to risk developing a fever. She had to stay well and rested. With a sigh of regret she turned back towards the villa.

And saw her maid Susannah standing waiting for her at the top of the veranda steps.

Immediately, Olivia felt a twinge of anxiety. She didn't know why. It wasn't as if she and the West Indian woman were close friends. But there was a rapport between them that Olivia had sensed as soon as she'd met her, and, recognising the agitation in the woman's dark-skinned face now, she couldn't help the sudden quiver in her stomach.

'Is something wrong?' she called, quickening her step, and Susannah moved aside to allow her to step up onto the veranda.

'Um—no, ma'am,' she said, but her tone was hardly convincing. Her hands twisted together at her waist. 'You got a phone call, Mrs Mora. From the States. I wasn't sure you'd want to take it.'

Olivia's jaw dropped. 'A phone call?' she echoed, her voice hardly louder than a whisper. Susannah knew that no one else knew she was here. Or rather,

Olivia had believed they didn't, she amended tensely. 'I—who is it?'

The housekeeper viewed her sympathetically. 'I think he said his name was Roderick or Rodrigo. Do you want me to tell him you're not here?'

Olivia's nails dug into her palms. Not Roderick or Rodrigo, she guessed. 'Could it have been Rodrigues?' she queried, hoping she didn't sound as panicked as she felt, and Susannah nodded with some relief.

'It could be,' she said. 'Do you know him?'

Olivia winced. Did she know Christian? In the biblical sense definitely, she thought, though that was almost laughable. Oh, God, she should have known she'd escaped too easily. She should have realised that Christian would track her down.

'I can find out what he wants?' offered Susannah, clearly a little concerned at Olivia's manner. In the eight weeks since she'd come to work for her, there had been no phone calls from the United States or anywhere else.

Olivia was tempted. The idea of letting Susannah deal with the call was appealing. She *didn't* have to explain herself to Christian. He wasn't Tony. He wasn't even a friend, she thought tensely. He had no right to hound her like this.

But then common sense reasserted itself. Did she want him to think she was afraid of him? Afraid to speak to him?

No!

'It's—all right, Susannah,' she managed to say now, reinforcing her words with a rueful smile. 'It's just a business associate of my late husband's.' Yeah, right.

'If you're sure?'

Susannah still looked doubtful and Olivia was warmed by the concern she could see in the other woman's face. 'I'm sure,' she said, taking a deep breath before stepping into the light and airy living room of the villa. 'Perhaps you could get me a glass of iced tea? I'm very thirsty.'

'Yes, ma'am.'

Susannah turned into the long passageway that ran from front to back of the sprawling residence while Olivia reluctantly approached the phone. It was lying on its side on an end table beside one of the three oatmeal leather sofas that formed a three-sided square before the flower-filled fireplace. With the windows open, the scent of blooms drifted irresistibly to Olivia's nostrils. She took another steadying breath before picking up the receiver.

'Yes?' she said, feigning ignorance. 'Who is this?'

'It's Christian Rodrigues,' he responded shortly, as if she knew any number of men with the same last name. 'Hello, Olivia. How are you?'

Olivia's teeth clenched. Did he expect her to answer him? Dammit, what the hell was he doing calling her here?

'What do you want, Christian?' she asked coldly, refusing to give him the satisfaction of humouring him. And then, because she couldn't resist asking, 'How did you know where to reach me?'

There was silence for a moment and she guessed he hadn't liked her reply. Then he said, his accent thickening as it always did when he was angry—or aroused, 'Oh, *por favor*, Olivia. Credit me with a little intelligence.'

Olivia's nails dug into the soft leather arm of the

sofa as she sank down onto its cushions. 'You knew where I was,' she said, the inflection a statement, not a question, and he sighed.

'You are Antonio Mora's widow, Olivia,' he said flatly. 'A wealthy woman in her own right. I owe it to Tony to look out for you. What kind of a man would I be if I betrayed his trust?'

Olivia's lips tightened. 'You tell me.'

Another silence, this time more hostile than the last, and she knew she had touched a nerve. Then, 'This is not the time to discuss the past, Olivia,' he told her harshly. And she didn't have to see his face to know he was angry now. 'But Tony is dead and, whether you like it or not, you are vulnerable. It is my responsibility to ensure that you are not disturbed in any way.'

'Except by you.'

She heard his sudden intake of breath and knew a moment's fear that she had gone too far. Christian had been a good friend to Tony but he would make a bad enemy. For her own sake—and for the sake of her child—she had to make him understand that she didn't need his help.

But how?

Taking another deep breath, she plunged into an impromptu explanation. 'Look, I'm sorry if I seem ungrateful, Christian, but you have to understand I was hoping for some privacy here. When—when Tony died, I didn't seem to have a minute to myself. Perhaps I was naïve in thinking I could get away without telling anyone where I was going. But I hope this doesn't mean I have to report to you every time I want to—want to—'

The words 'take a leak' seemed most appropriate,

but this time she bit her tongue before she offended him again. Somehow, she had to convince him that she was all right, that she needed nothing from him. If she could just keep her head, he would soon realise he was wasting his time with her.

'I do not expect you to report to me at all, Olivia,' he said now, almost grimly, and her heart sank at the thought that perhaps he wasn't going to be so easy to dismiss after all. 'But it would have been a courtesy to leave your forwarding address with my secretary.'

Not likely! Olivia's mouth tightened. She refused to give that promiscuous bitch the time of day. Dolores Samuels had been trying to get her claws into Christian ever since Tony had blown her off a year ago. He must know that. Or had he already availed himself of her far-too-obvious allure?

The idea should not have been so distasteful to her and to cover herself, she muttered, 'Perhaps I should.' But she resented his assumption that she owed him any explanations. Dammit, he wasn't her husband. She owed him nothing at all.

'I'm sorry if you feel I have overstepped my position, Olivia,' he declared into the silence that had followed her reluctant submission. 'But, in the circumstances, it was—unavoidable.'

Unavoidable? Olivia stiffened. Was she missing something here? Surely he couldn't have found out about— But, no. That was impossible. She'd told no one she was seeing a doctor and a patient's records were confidential, weren't they?

She shook her head. She was being paranoid. She'd done nothing to arouse anyone's suspicions, least of all his. Whatever he wanted, it had to be something to do with Tony's estate. But why hadn't he contacted Luis? Was the power Tony had given him not enough?

'I don't understand,' she said now, adopting an aloof tone. 'What is—*was*—unavoidable?'

'Luis is in hospital in San Francisco,' replied Christian without preamble, and Olivia was glad she was sitting down when he threw that at her.

'In hospital?' she echoed weakly, her hand clammy on the receiver. 'Oh, God, what's happened? Is he ill?'

'Not ill, no,' responded Christian swiftly, and she guessed he wasn't totally insensitive to her feelings. 'His car ploughed into a wall. Luis was driving, naturally. He has a fractured pelvis, bruises, concussion...' he paused '...and initially a suspected broken neck.'

The whimper of pain Olivia gave was audible to him and she heard Christian utter a frustrated imprecation. Then, almost savagely, he said, 'He is not dying, Olivia. His spine was bruised, that is all. There is no fracture. With time—and the skill of his doctors—he should recover completely.'

Olivia swallowed. 'You're sure of that?'

'As sure as I can be.' Christian expelled a sharp breath. 'I am not an expert, Olivia. But my understanding is that your precious boy will soon be as good as new.'

Olivia stiffened. 'You needn't be sarcastic, Christian. I realise that both you and Tony were born with balance sheets clutched in your power-hungry little hands. But Luis isn't like that. He realises there's more to life than money.'

'*Vale.*' The ice in Christian's voice was almost palpable. 'I suppose that is why he was only driving a Porsche Turbo instead of the GT?'

Olivia pressed her lips together. 'Just tell me where he is,' she said coldly. 'I want to go and see him.'

'There is no need.'

'What do you mean, there is no need?' Olivia was infuriated, her earlier panic giving way to indignation at his words. 'Which hospital was he taken to? You might as well tell me. Because if you don't, I will find out—'

'Cool it, will you?' Christian's tone was flat now.

Olivia wished she didn't feel so helpless. 'You can't stop me seeing him, Christian.'

'God!' His exclamation was fervent. 'I am not trying to stop you from seeing him, Olivia. But there's no need for you to think about flying out to San Francisco when I've arranged for him to be flown back to Miami in the morning.'

Olivia gasped. 'You've what?' She couldn't believe it.

'I think you heard me, Olivia.'

'But—' She struggled for words. 'You had no right to do that.'

'No?'

'No,' she spluttered. 'It's too soon for him to be moved. You said he has a fractured pelvis. He probably has whiplash. And what about the concussion—?'

'The mild concussion?' he inquired evenly and she wanted to scream. 'He will survive.'

'I still think you shouldn't have made the decision to move him,' she declared hotly. 'Just because you can't be bothered to take time off from your personal schedule to go and see him, you're prepared to risk possible complications to satisfy your own ends.'

'That's your opinion, is it?'

He was breathing heavily now. She could hear it, and for a moment she was tempted to say nothing more. But she couldn't let him intimidate her and, squaring her shoulders, she said, 'Yes, it is.' She paused and then added defensively, 'And whatever his faults, I'm sure it would have been Tony's opinion as well.'

'You think?' He blew out a breath and, although she couldn't see him, she sensed the anger that was simmering just beneath his iron control. 'Well, *querida*, for your information, Luis's doctor has assessed his condition and sanctioned the transfer to the hospital in Miami. An air ambulance, fully equipped with both doctors and nursing staff, will fly him from the local airport in San Francisco. Subsequently, he will be airlifted to the Sacred Heart. Does that reassure you?'

Olivia moistened her lips. 'I—I suppose it has to.'

'Good.' But he was sardonic. 'Then that only leaves us with the question of when you will come to Miami to visit him.'

Oh, God! Olivia sank back against the soft leather. She'd known it was coming, of course, but it sounded so much more ominous when he said it.

'You—you say Luis is being flown back to Miami tomorrow?' she asked, prevaricating, and Christian agreed.

'Naturally, with the time change, you would be advised not to try and see him until the day after,' he observed drily. 'I suggest I send a helicopter for you on Thursday morning. If you can be ready for, say, ten-thirty, we could—'

'I don't need your help to get back to Miami,' Olivia interrupted him swiftly. The idea of Christian coming here, invading her sanctuary, didn't bear thinking about. 'I can get a flight myself.'

'When?' Christian sounded impatient. 'Come on, Olivia, we both know that you've got to get from San Gimeno to New Providence before you can even think about taking a flight.'

'There are such things as charter flights,' she retorted, desperate to avoid his intervention. 'I do have the money to hire a pilot, you know.'

'But why should you want to do that when the Mora Corporation owns a couple of choppers?' demanded Christian infuriatedly. 'If what you're really saying is that you don't want me to escort you, then okay. I'll have Mike Delano make the trip.'

'There's no need for you to send anyone,' she persisted, but now she had gone too far.

'Forget it, Olivia,' he said harshly. 'So far I've managed to keep this under wraps, but once you start hiring a plane to get back here, someone's going to find out. I accept that you don't like me. *Dios*, I've known that for the past eight years. And yes, what happened the night Tony died was unforgivable and you're not going to let me forget it. Well, okay. I can live with that. I won't insult you by saying you wanted it as much as me. But this—this is something different. We've got to protect Luis from the kind of publicity this is going to create. After what happened when his father died, I'd have thought you'd have wanted that, too. Luis is the only son you've got.'

For a heart-stopping moment Olivia wondered what

he'd do if he found out why she'd run away. Convincing Luis that she'd needed some time alone to get over his father's death had been easy. Convincing Christian of the same was something else.

His next words reassured her, however. 'Look, Olivia,' he said. 'I'm not asking you to do this for me.'

I know. She quivered.

'But Luis will expect to see you,' he continued. 'He has talked of little else since he recovered consciousness.'

Olivia expelled an unsteady breath. 'Well, naturally I want to see him, too—'

'So do the sensible thing and let me send the helicopter for you.'

Olivia hesitated. 'On Thursday morning?'

'Yes.'

She shook her head. In his eyes, it seemed so simple. And wasn't she running the risk of arousing his suspicions by persisting in arguing with him now?

And yet...

'I'll think about it,' she said at last, knowing he would take that as an acceptance, and rang off before he could ask her anything else.

CHAPTER TWO

IT WAS raining.

It didn't often rain in Miami, but when it did it was usually a downpour. The present downpour was courtesy of Hurricane Flora, which had been downgraded to a tropical storm before it reached the mainland. It was probably the last hurricane of the season, but that didn't make it any the less unpleasant. Nor did it improve Christian Rodrigues's temper as he strode from his car into the Mora Building, brushing the drops of water from the shoulders of his fine wool Italian suit.

Thankfully, the hurricane hadn't touched the Bahamas. It had come in over the Gulf of Mexico and dissipated itself in the islands that bordered the gulf coast. There was no reason why Olivia's flight should have been delayed or for her to make any excuse for not flying. Yet the helicopter had come back without her and, although he'd tried to reach her by other means, she apparently wasn't answering her phone.

He strode across the marble lobby, taking little notice of its arching roof or the exquisite examples of glass and artwork that gave the space its elegant appeal. A dozen journals had praised its architectural brilliance, but on this dull Thursday morning Christian was in little mood to appreciate his surroundings.

Or his own success in working there. Antonio Mora had been his father's cousin and when he'd invited the much younger Christian to come and work for him it had been a marvellous opportunity. Christian had been in college then, working for a law degree and holding down two part-time jobs just to pay for his tuition fees. His parents were dead, killed in a landslide while they were visiting his grandparents in Venezuela, and until Antonio—Tony—came on the scene, Christian had never thought of contacting his distant relative.

But Tony had just heard that his cousin was dead and he wanted to help. He'd offered to pay Christian's tuition fees himself if Christian agreed to come and work for him after he'd graduated. He wanted to do something in his cousin's memory, he'd said, and although the boy had bought it at the time, Christian had learned better since.

Tony had done nothing for nothing. Despite the fact that he'd rarely visited his cousin and his family, he'd apparently been impressed by Christian's intelligence. Tony had needed someone he could trust, someone he could rely on. Family had meant a lot to Tony, and until Luis was older he'd wanted someone of his own blood to be his second-in-command.

Maybe, too, he'd already realised that Luis wasn't like him. He was more like his mother—or rather his stepmother, Christian had soon decided. The cool and lovely Mrs Mora, who had never liked him; who had always regarded him with a scarcely veiled contempt, as if she thought she knew exactly why he'd accepted Tony's offer and it had nothing to do with either gratitude or family ties.

That she was wrong, but that there was nothing he could do to change her mind, was something he'd learned to live with. Besides, Olivia Mora had had a lot more to contend with than his annoying presence.

Within a few weeks of coming to work for Tony he'd discovered that her marriage was as hollow as her husband's promises. Tony Mora had been congenitally incapable of being faithful to any woman. If Olivia was suspicious of Christian it was probably because she'd learned to be suspicious of all men.

He'd also known that however careless Tony had been of his vows, he would have killed anyone who touched his Olivia. And Christian had more sense than to look her way. Besides which, despite Tony's infidelities, she had seemed contented enough. Luis appeared to satisfy all her needs.

Or he had, brooded Christian grimly, affording the smiling receptionists, who occupied the huge slab of plate glass that passed for a desk in the lobby, only a grunted greeting. So why the hell hadn't she been on board the helicopter when it had landed at the airport?

Despite her unwillingness to accept his help, he'd gone to meet her himself, deciding it would be better if they got any unpleasantness over with before they got to the hospital. He didn't think she'd say anything in front of Luis. But the boy might detect the animosity between them and wonder why.

Christian scowled. Instead of that the helicopter had come back empty. The pilot had offered the excuse that she hadn't turned up at the small airstrip. He hadn't been able to wait around indefinitely. He had other commitments that day.

But why wasn't she answering her phone? Christian stepped into one of the half dozen elevators that gave access to the upper floors of the building and punched the button for the forty-second floor with unnecessary force. She must have known he'd try to get in touch with her when she wasn't on board the helicopter. Dammit, what the hell was going on?

His secretary, Dolores Samuels, met him in the foyer of his suite of offices and he guessed his presence in the building had been duly reported. Small and dark and fiery, Dolores showed her Latin heritage in every excitable movement she made, and her hands fluttered expressively when she saw his glowering face.

'She was not on the flight?' she asked, her dark eyes wide and knowing, and Christian stared at her.

'How do you know that?'

Dolores's tongue circled her lips in deliberate invitation. 'Because Mike Delano called from the hospital,' she replied slyly. 'Mrs Mora arrived there only minutes after you left for the airport.'

Christian's jaw compressed. 'So why didn't you ring me?' he demanded, turning back towards the corridor outside his room with obvious intent. 'It would have saved me the trip.'

'Because she told Mike not to tell you,' Dolores protested, her expression turning from artful teasing to innocent appeal in a moment. 'You know what they say?' She snapped her fingers. 'Don't kill the messenger. I am only telling you what Mike Delano said when he phoned a few minutes ago.'

'Since when does Mike Delano take his orders from Mrs Mora?' retorted Christian grimly. 'And why didn't he ring me instead of you?'

'I expect because he knew you would turn around and go straight to the hospital,' exclaimed Dolores, tugging beguilingly on a strand of curling dark hair. 'And she is Luis's mother. She didn't want you to interfere.'

'She's his *step*mother,' Christian corrected her shortly, and Dolores's eyes grew even wider at his aggravated tone.

'Does it matter?' she asked. 'She is old. And she is Tony's widow. I expect Mike was too intimidated to ignore what she said.'

Christian didn't know why he felt so infuriated by her argument, but he did. 'Olivia is not old,' he said. 'She is—what? Thirty-seven? Thirty-eight? That is not old, Dolores.'

'It is to me,' retorted the girl sulkily. 'And to you, too, *no esta*?' She paused, regarding him curiously. 'Do not tell me you are interested in the frozen widow.'

Christian realised this was becoming too personal. Dolores had tried to engage him in conversations like this before and he had always put her off. She was too inquisitive, too provocative, and she was a gossip. And since the break-up of the affair she'd had with Tony she'd renewed her pursuit of her present boss with an increasingly flagrant intent.

'I do not think Mrs Mora would appreciate your assessment of her character,' he replied obliquely. He had no intention of discussing his association with his late cousin's wife with her. 'I suggest you confine yourself to business matters in the future. You are a good assistant, Dolores, but that is the only reason I persuaded Tony to let you keep your job.'

Dolores's full lips pursed. 'If you say so,' she remarked insolently, turning back into her office, and it was only because he was in a hurry to get to the hospital that Christian chose not to challenge her again. But one day he would have to deal with her.

He wanted no one to speculate about his efforts on her behalf.

With a gesture of frustration, he pulled out his cell-phone and ordered his chauffeur to bring his car up from the basement garage. Then he walked swiftly back to the elevator.

Sacred Heart Hospital was situated in downtown Miami and long before he reached the quiet enclave off Flagler Street, Christian's car was snarled in traffic. Perhaps he should have arranged for Luis to be transferred to a hospital north of Miami, he reflected irritably, drumming his fingers against the steering wheel. He'd chosen to dismiss his chauffeur and drive himself and now, with the rain sluicing against the windscreen and the fumes from countless other vehicles invading the car, he was feeling decidedly put-upon.

Why the hell had Olivia chosen to make her own way to the hospital? he wondered, returning to his earlier gripe. Was it her way of proving she wanted nothing more to do with him? Or was it badness that had prompted her to thwart his plans?

His jaw hardened. She was going to have to deal with him sooner or later. He was one of the executors of the trust that was going to keep her in luxury for the rest of her life. If she didn't like it, tough. It wasn't her decision. However she felt about it, that was the way it was going to be.

It was early afternoon by the time he entered the hospital's car park. It was full, but after a brief altercation with the uniformed security guard, which entailed a hundred-dollar bill changing hands, he was allowed to park in a space designated for staff members only. Then, after getting another soaking crossing to the entrance, he at last reached the lobby of the brightly lit establishment.

He had to run the gamut of more security checks before being allowed to take the stairs to the second floor. There were elevators, but they were all busy, and he was too impatient to wait while wheelchair-bound patients and porters wheeling gurneys took precedence. Besides, he expunged some of his frustrated energies in the act, reaching Luis's door before he had himself totally in control.

Olivia was sitting beside her stepson's bed, her hand resting lightly on his where it lay upon the coverlet. She was leaning towards him, speaking softly, when Christian opened the door, and the intimacy of the scene he was interrupting was not lost on him.

There was no sign of Mike Delano, but that didn't surprise him. If Olivia had prevailed on Mike not to call his employer, the man was hardly likely to be hanging around here. He was probably downstairs in the coffee shop, drowning his sorrows in a double-cream cappuccino.

Christian would speak to him later, but for now he had to contend with a pair of clear grey eyes regarding him with undisguised irritation. Olivia was annoyed; that much was obvious. But he was bloody annoyed, too, and he refused to be daunted by the cool resentment in her gaze.

'Hi,' he said crisply, his eyes moving past her to the young man in the bed. 'Luis.' His thin lips formed a smile. 'How are you feeling?'

'I'm okay.' Luis managed to return his greeting but his face was still drawn with pain. He looked very pale, Christian thought, his tanned skin bleached al-

most to the colour of the sheet behind his head.
'Thanks.'

'Good.' Christian came to stand across the bed
from Olivia, forcing himself to concentrate on its oc-
cupant and not on her. 'No after-effects of the flight?'

'Just a bit of jet lag, I guess,' said Luis bravely. 'I
appreciate you coming with me, Chris. It was good
to see a friendly face among all those white coats.'

Christian's smile flattened, but he was aware that
Olivia flicked a glance at him before turning to her
stepson again. 'You didn't tell me—Christian had es-
corted you back to Miami, Luis,' she said, her nor-
mally husky voice sharpening with confusion. 'You
know I would have flown back with you myself if I'd
known what was going on.'

Once again she afforded Christian a resentful look,
but before he could speak Luis intervened. 'Oh—
Chris flew up the day after I had the accident,' he
explained, and Christian saw the way the hand lying
in Olivia's lap balled into a fist at his words. 'He
stayed with me until the doctors said he could arrange
the transfer. That was how we flew back together.'

Olivia looked as if she was about to object, but this
time Christian beat her to it. 'I phoned you from San
Francisco,' he explained, meeting her taut gaze with
some satisfaction. 'I thought you realised that.'

He knew she hadn't, and she knew he was lying,
too, judging by the angry tightening of her soft
mouth. Christian scowled. Now where had that come
from? Her mouth was anything but soft at this moment. It was fairly trembling with the indignation she
was trying so hard to suppress.

But, 'No,' was all she said in answer, before returning her attention to the young man in the bed.

'Well, I'm glad Christian was there to look after you. I expect he realised how worried I'd have been if I'd known what was going on.'

'Yeah.' Luis turned grateful eyes to the older man again. 'Chris's been great. He hasn't even moaned about me wrecking the Porsche.'

'That's not to say I won't,' put in Christian drily. 'Especially if it turns out you were driving stoned out of your skull. I think you need a safer motor. I'm thinking about buying you a bug next time.'

'If I ever drive again,' muttered Luis, tears suddenly forming at the corners of his eyes, and Olivia made a sound of impatience as she gripped the boy's hand with both of hers.

'Of course you'll drive again,' she said, using her thumb to smear his tears away. She gave Christian another speaking appraisal. 'Don't you agree?'

'Sure.' Christian agreed with her. He brushed a hand across the boy's shoulder and gave him a rueful smile. 'So long as you do what you're told and don't give the doctors any grief,' he added gently. 'I know you feel pretty desperate now, kid, but it's amazing what a few weeks' bed-rest can achieve.'

'You think?'

Luis sniffed and Christian was half relieved when he heard the door open behind him and a white-clad nurse entered the room. 'I'm afraid you'll have to leave now,' she said, softening her words with a warm smile for her patient. 'It's time for Luis's evaluation. Dr Hoffman is waiting for him. I'm going to wheel him along to the examination suite, okay?'

Olivia got immediately to her feet and Christian was instantly made aware of how tall and slender she was. Her hair, which was a shade between honey and silver, was secured at her nape with a leather thong, and the gold loops in her ears drew his attention to the delicate curve of her neck.

But he also noticed that although she was wearing a cream, ruched silk shirt, that complemented her slight tan and was only loosely tucked into her waistband, she was wearing it with low-waisted jeans and not one of the designer suits he was used to seeing. A small change, perhaps, but a significant one, and he wondered if her attitude towards him was all part of some determined desire to show she could look after herself.

Whatever, she looked coolly elegant and Christian wished she weren't regarding him with such an expression of contempt. All right, he knew he'd made a mistake; a big one. But if she hadn't been so willing, he would never have let it go so far.

A grimness tugged at the corner of his mouth and it was a struggle to smile at Luis as if nothing were wrong. 'See you later, kid,' he said as an orderly came to assist the nurse in moving the boy's bed. 'And I'll get something organised, like I promised. You're not going to have to stay in here any longer than is absolutely necessary, right?'

'Right,' murmured Luis, but his face was despondent, and Olivia moved forward to take his hand again.

'Just know I'm here for you,' she said, bending to bestow a butterfly kiss on his temple. 'Don't worry, darling. You're going to be okay.'

Olivia followed Luis's bed out into the corridor and stood watching as the nursing staff wheeled it away. Then, as if realising she couldn't ignore him indefinitely, she cast a brief look at Christian and said, 'Excuse me. I'm going to go and get a coffee.'

Christian jammed his hands into the pockets of his jacket, resisting the urge to grab her by the shoulders and hold her where she was. Did she honestly think she could get away with what she'd done so lightly? Had she any conception of how bloody angry he was?

Controlling his temper, he said, 'I'll join you,' and although he was sure she wanted to object, a slight shrug of her shoulders was all the response he got.

She made for the bank of lifts and Christian had to stifle his frustration and stay with her. And, even though an influx of staff and visitors and patients made the downward trip an ordeal, they eventually reached the basement and the hospital cafeteria.

Thankfully, it wasn't busy. Nor was there any sign of Mike Delano, which was a relief. At this hour of the afternoon, the lunch crowd had gone and the evening rush hadn't started. Nevertheless, the smells emanating from the kitchens reminded Christian that he hadn't eaten since breakfast. Deciding he owed Olivia no favours, he ordered a cheeseburger and fries to go with his coffee.

'What can I get you?' he asked, beating her to the self-service counter, and she gave him a frosty look.

'Just coffee,' she said, clearly wishing she didn't have to accept his hospitality, and Christian nodded his acknowledgement as she went to find a table.

By the time he carried his tray across to where she was waiting, Olivia's impatience was obvious in the way she was shifting restlessly in her seat. She'd chosen a table in the centre of the room, probably to deter him from thinking this was in any way a friendly encounter, but her expression changed when she saw what was on the tray.

Christian wasn't sure, but he thought she paled slightly, and her breathing quickened, drawing his attention to the dusky hollow visible in the open neckline of her shirt. Silken ties hung loose and she clutched them with nervous fingers. Pale fabric lay against her golden skin, a sensuous invitation he couldn't ignore.

'Is something wrong?' he queried, taking the chair opposite so she couldn't accuse him of crowding her. He unloaded the plate containing the burger and fries onto the table. 'Are you sure I can't get you something to eat?'

'No.'

She waved a hand in front of her face and he got the impression she was trying to waft the smell of the food away. Well, it wasn't his fault if she felt sick with hunger, he assured himself. She probably hadn't had any lunch, either, and there was no sense in starving herself to spite him.

Shrugging, he picked up his burger and took a generous bite. It was years since he'd lived on junk food but the juicy flavour of the meat reminded him irresistibly of his student days. And of the first time he'd seen his cousin's wife...

Realising she was not about to speak to him—indeed, had half turned away from him, as if watching him eat his food was actually distasteful to her—Christian emptied his mouth.

'Perhaps you'd like to tell me why you rejected the use of the helicopter,' he said mildly. 'Or if not that, then at least explain why you couldn't have called and saved the pilot a useless trip.'

Olivia blew out a breath and, without looking at him, she said, 'I knew you wouldn't take no for an answer.' She swallowed a little convulsively and then added faintly, 'I'd already tried to tell you I didn't need your help.'

Christian felt angry enough to swear in his own language. It annoyed him like hell that Olivia could make him lose his temper like this. 'The helicopter is not mine. It belongs to the Mora Corporation. You are just as entitled to use it as me.'

'Does it matter?'

Once again, Olivia wafted her hand across her face and Christian noticed the film of sweat on her upper lip. She hadn't even touched her coffee. For pity's sake, he thought irritably, couldn't they even have a civil conversation?

'It matters,' he said now, pushing the burger aside, suddenly as uninterested in the food as she was. 'Look, are we going to have to spend the next God knows how many years fencing around what's really going on here? You don't like me, Olivia. Well, here's a newsflash, I'm not madly keen on you, either. But we've got to work together. Can't we at least call a truce?'

Olivia's gaze turned to him, but where he'd expected to see hostility he glimpsed only panic. 'Where are the rest rooms?' she choked, a hand over her mouth almost making her words indistinguishable, and as he cast around for an answer she left the table and rushed headlong out of the restaurant.

He followed her, of course, but he was too late to be of any help. By the time he reached the corridor, she was disappearing through the door marked

'Women'. He expelled a frustrated sigh and was forced to kick his heels outside until she came out.

It seemed an age before she reappeared again, although he guessed it had only been a few minutes. She emerged looking even paler, her eyes pink-rimmed and a visible redness around her mouth.

She'd been sick. That much was obvious to him. Dammit, he hadn't realised Luis's accident would upset her so much. He straightened away from the wall where he'd been lounging and regarded her with some concern. 'Are you all right?'

Clearly, she wasn't, but she made a brave effort to pretend she was. 'It must have been something I ate,' she said, making no attempt to disguise what had happened. 'And seeing Luis.' She rubbed her lips again with the tissue she'd brought out of the rest room with her. 'I suppose I didn't expect all that bracing around his neck.'

'I'm told they have to immobilise the neck to prevent further injury,' said Christian gently. 'It's just a cervical collar. As I told you, his spine isn't injured.'

'All the same—'

'Olivia, he's not paralysed. He feels bad, I grant you. I dare say his hip isn't very comfortable right now. But he will get better.' He grimaced. 'The doctors in San Francisco were very thorough. They seemed to think he'd been very lucky.'

Olivia bit her lip. 'He says he doesn't have a lot of pain,' she murmured and Christian nodded.

'And he hasn't needed any surgery at all.'

'Any surgery?'

She was staring at him with wide eyes and Christian cursed himself for mentioning it. 'There can be internal injuries after a car crash,' he told her un-willingly. 'But Luis has no internal bleeding at all.'

'Thank God.'

'Indeed. A few weeks' rest and he'll be back on his feet, as good as new.'

'You think so?'

Christian nodded. 'I do.'

She shook her head. 'Dear God, what if—?'

'Olivia, we can all torture ourselves with ''what-ifs'',' he declared flatly. 'What if he hadn't been driving so fast? What if he hadn't been on that particular stretch of highway at all? He did, he was, and this has happened. It's up to us to make it as easy as possible for him to get over it. Right?'

She sniffed and then said stiffly, 'Us?'

'Yeah.' Christian glanced back into the cafeteria. 'Look, why don't we go and sit down again?'

'Not in there.' Her response was urgent, and she turned her face away from the restaurant. 'I—perhaps we should go back upstairs. Luis may be back from his examination by now.'

'And he may not,' retorted Christian shortly. 'Come on, Olivia. We've got to talk about this so it might as well be now.' He chewed on his lip for a moment, and then added, 'Why don't we go and find a lounge? There are bound to be waiting rooms for visitors somewhere.'

She hesitated for a moment and he thought she was going to balk again, but she didn't. 'All right,' she agreed at last. 'You can tell me how the accident happened, and how you came to be the one they got in touch with.'

Christian's mouth flattened. Yeah, right, he thought grimly. That was the most important thing as far as she was concerned. What had happened months before the accident and how they were going to deal with that in the future was not in question. She was only talking to him at all because she really didn't have a choice.

They took the stairs instead of using the elevator. Evidently, Olivia had no desire to be confined in an airless cubicle where the smell of antiseptic and medication were all-pervading. In her present state, she would have probably preferred to walk outdoors, but that wasn't possible. Even without the rain, the streets beyond the parking lot that surrounded the hospital wouldn't offer them the privacy they sought.

They found a visitors' lounge on the second floor, just down the corridor from Luis's room. To Christian's relief, it was empty, though he guessed Olivia didn't share his enthusiasm as she surveyed the deserted chairs and sofas.

But there was a coffee machine in one corner and Christian got them both plastic cups of the steaming beverage before he sat down. Olivia, he saw, had chosen an armchair and he took the sofa opposite. He deposited the cups on the table nearby before spreading his legs and letting his hands hang loosely between his thighs.

He couldn't help but notice that she avoided looking at him. But she gave him a brief nod of thanks for the coffee before concentrating on the contents of the cup. With it cradled between her palms, she was successfully shutting him off from whatever thoughts she was entertaining. He guessed she wasn't only thinking about her stepson.

But he couldn't ask her that now. 'Okay,' he said instead, forcing her to listen to him. 'The first thing we have to decide is where Luis is going to convalesce when he leaves the hospital.'

That got her attention. The pinkness had left her lids now and long, silvery-grey eyes set between thick curling lashes focussed on his face. 'Where he's going to convalesce?' she echoed. 'Isn't that a little premature? We still don't know how long he's going to be in the hospital.'

'Not long,' said Christian, taking a mouthful of his own coffee. He found it palatable, if a little weak. 'It's my experience that patients who are not in need of any surgery are discharged fairly quickly. They're encouraged to continue their recovery at home.'

'At home?' Once again she repeated his words. 'But—Luis's apartment is at Berkeley. There's no one to care for him there.'

'I know that.' Christian put down his cup and regarded her intently. 'How would you feel about opening up the house in Bal Harbour and caring for him there? After all, it was Luis's home as well until he left for the west coast. I know you chose to leave Miami, but I don't suppose that's written in stone.'

CHAPTER THREE

IT IS.

Olivia's lips parted in dismay. She'd suspected what was coming, of course, but she still wasn't prepared for the shock she got when he voiced the words. He expected her to look after Luis. To go on being the mother she had been for the past fifteen years. But she couldn't. She couldn't. She couldn't come back to live in Bal Harbour. Not with Christian just a few miles away, able to come and go as often as he pleased.

And what about Luis himself? She'd hoped to have had the baby before she saw him again. It had been a faint hope, she knew, but since he'd gone to college Luis had become much less dependent on her. As she'd assumed no one knew where she was, it hadn't seemed such a stretch.

'I—can't,' she said now, before sympathy for her stepson and her own thwarted maternal instincts kicked in. She put her coffee cup down before she dropped it. 'I'd like to help Luis, but—well, coming back to Florida isn't on my agenda.'

Christian's dark face showed his angry reaction. Although he was not a handsome man, his strong features did possess a sensual appeal. A *sexual* appeal, she admitted, trying to avoid that conclusion and failing miserably. But at this moment any sensuality—or sexuality—was absent.

'What is on your agenda?' he demanded, and although she was tempted to tell him to mind his own business, she guarded her tongue.

'I have plans,' she said vaguely. Plans that did not include spending the next few months evading Christian's suspicions.

'What plans?' he asked at once, as she'd known he would, and she wondered if he realised how arrogant his question was.

Probably, she decided, giving his dark intense features a covert appraisal. Christian always knew exactly what he was doing. From the moment Tony had brought his cousin's orphaned son into the business, Christian had known precisely where he was going. He'd always intended to be Tony's successor, and now he was. But he had no right to push family obligations into her face.

A faint twinge of guilt rippled over her. Who was she to talk about family obligations when she had no intention of telling him she was expecting his child? She knew what he'd do if he ever found out about the baby and that was what scared her. He'd expect to play a prominent role in its life.

But the last thing she wanted was another marriage like the one she'd had with Tony. Okay, maybe she'd been naïve in thinking Tony had married her because he loved her, but she had expected some loyalty from him. Instead of which within weeks of her wedding she'd discovered he was still seeing the woman he'd been having an affair with before he'd asked Olivia to marry him. Tony had had no intention of changing his way of life. He'd enjoyed the excitement of the chase too much.

And Christian was like his cousin. He'd no doubt expect his wife to be as pure as the driven snow while

he slept with whomever he chose. Olivia had already
lost count of the number of girlfriends he'd had since
he came to work for Tony. He seemed to have as
little respect for her sex as Tony had himself.

Of course, she was flattering herself by thinking
that Christian might ask her to marry him. Heavens,
she was at least six years older than he was and that
was a lot. Just because she was having his baby she
should not think he'd consider giving up his freedom
for her. Yet, like his cousin, he cared about family.
He might be willing to sacrifice his freedom to give
his child a name.

Oh, God, if only it had been anyone other than
Christian who had brought her the news about Tony.
Even now, she found it hard to believe that she'd
behaved as she had. She'd been a reckless fool and
now she had to deal with it. Which meant, if she
wanted to maintain her independence, keeping him
from finding out she was having his child.

Realising he was waiting for her answer, she decided to tell him part of the truth and risk his derision.
'I—I want to write and illustrate children's books,'
she said quickly, resenting the need to bare her soul
to him. 'It's what I've always wanted to do, but—
well, I've never had the time before.'

'No?' Christian's dark brows arched quizzically
and he gave her a disbelieving look.

'No.' She disliked his attitude. 'No, I haven't.'

'I see.' His lips twisted into a mocking smirk. 'And
you've been busy doing—what, exactly?'

'I don't think that's any of your business,' she retorted, refusing to try and explain her reasons to him.
'Anyway, those are my plans.'

'And all these years you've been married to Tony,

you've never found the time to put pen to paper before?'

Olivia's mouth tightened. 'Not seriously, no.'

Christian picked up his cup again and took another mouthful of the cooling coffee. But his eyes continued to survey her across the rim of his cup. She felt her pulse quicken, her palms grow damp with apprehension. He was no fool, she thought uneasily, and he must be wondering where she should have suddenly acquired this desire to write.

Nevertheless, while Tony was alive such an activity would have been unthinkable. Despite his own shortcomings, Tony had never allowed her to forget that she was his wife, his possession. He'd given her total freedom with his son, but in all other respects she'd been expected to comply with his wishes. And, for Luis's sake, she'd stifled her own ambitions, contenting herself with making up stories for the boy and illustrating them in his drawing books.

Christian put down his cup with a measured deliberation and Olivia stiffened instinctively. What now? she wondered, watching as he smoothed long brown fingers over the fine woollen cloth that lovingly encased his thigh. He was wearing one of the Italian-designed suits he generally favoured, its charcoal fabric complementing and enhancing his virile appeal.

His dark features were potently male, too, and she was not unaware of it. Nor was she unaware that the hands that were presently employed in such an apparently innocent activity had once caressed her skin. She remembered how it had felt when he'd peeled her nightgown from her, how hotly sensual his skin had felt against her bare flesh...

'*Lo que sea*,' he said, with a shrug, but she knew

it was a measure of his frustration that he'd spoken in his own language. He'd spoken Spanish when he was making love to her, she remembered, the unwilling memory of his hands pushing into her hair, of his mouth playing with hers, of the awareness that had started deep within her abdomen and spread to every tingling nerve in her body, causing her to press her hot palms against her suddenly burning cheeks.

But Christian hadn't made love to her, she corrected herself fiercely. What they'd shared had been hot and carnal, but love had had nothing to do with it. They'd had sex, pure and simple. Good sex, perhaps; great sex, she admitted honestly. Not that she was any expert. Tony had been the first and only man she'd slept with.

Until Christian...

Why had he done such a thing? she asked herself again, as she'd asked so many times before. Christian didn't take risks. He was far too astute for that. In all his dealings with the women he had dated, there had never been a paternity suit raised against him. Yet he'd made love to her without taking any precautions. Hadn't he ever considered that there might be a price to pay for his neglect?

The only solution was that he had been in as much of a state of shock as she was, when a desire to celebrate life had followed the reality of Tony's death. Or had he needed comfort, too? Someone to cling to? She doubted she would ever know.

She removed her hands from her cheeks and made a play of repositioning her coffee-cup. He'd evidently assumed she was taking some form of birth-control pill. After all, she and Tony hadn't had any children of their own. He couldn't know that she and Tony hadn't slept together for years. Or that she'd discovered Tony had had a vasectomy soon after Luis was born.

Her shoulders moved now in an involuntary gesture. It had been quite a blow when she'd found out. Despite Tony's unfaithfulness, she had wanted a baby of her own. Some compensation, perhaps, for the hollowness of her existence.

But that was all a long time ago now. She'd got over it and there was no denying that Luis loved her more than the mother who had died at his birth. Yet she also knew it was the reason Tony had gone looking for Christian after his parents were killed in Venezuela. It had reminded him of his own mortality and of how arbitrary death could be.

'So—will you tell Luis or do you wish me to do it?' Christian asked abruptly, startling her out of her reverie. 'He'll be disappointed, *no*? But if you have no objections to him staying at the house in Bal Harbour, I will arrange for full-time nursing staff to look after him.'

Olivia stared at him now. *Bastard*, she thought resentfully. He must know how she'd feel about leaving her stepson to the mercies of people he neither knew nor cared about. But what could she do? She couldn't come back to Florida. There had to be a way to satisfy his demands without losing her self-respect.

'Olivia?'

His dark eyes were watching her closely and she very much wanted to avert her own from his penetrating gaze. But to do so would simply reinforce his smug belief that he had the upper hand. And she was damned if she was going to give in without a fight.

'Let me think about it,' she said at last, and, although his lashes swept down to hide his expression, she glimpsed the triumph in his face. 'I'm not promising anything,' she added, stung into a retort, and he inclined his head.

'I am sure inspiration would strike you just as successfully in Bal Harbour as in San Gimeno,' he remarked smoothly, and once again she flinched at his condescending tone.

'You're sure of that, are you?' she countered, arching her brows in imitation of his. 'Well, that's some compensation anyway. I'm glad I have your support.'

Christian's mouth tightened. 'I do not wish to quarrel with you, Olivia,' he said. 'You seem to have the mistaken impression that I am enjoying this. Let me assure you, I am not. But Luis is my cousin's only child. Naturally, I am concerned that he has the best attention possible.'

'Why don't you look after him, then?'

Olivia knew her response was childish but she couldn't help it. He expected her to sacrifice any plans she'd made for the future. Would he be as willing to do the same? It would certainly put a crimp in his social calendar, she thought, her soft mouth tightening. And, in truth, Christian's connection to Luis was far closer than hers could ever be.

There was silence for a few moments and then he expelled a long sigh. 'I assume you are suggesting that I move into the Bal Harbour house, too?' he queried. 'You would have no problem with that arrangement?'

Olivia did have a problem with it, but she could hardly say that now. 'Why should I?' she asked, deciding to call his bluff, and Christian frowned before going on.

'So you would be happy to visit him there?' he persisted and she shrugged.

'Why not?'

'Indeed.' He was thoughtful. 'So the reason you've abandoned your home and taken refuge on some primitive island has nothing to do with what happened between us?'

Olivia was taken aback. 'I—of course not.'

'No?' Christian regarded her between narrowed lids. 'You are sure about that?'

Olivia struggled to remain calm. He knew nothing, she reminded herself. This was just another attempt to bait her, that was all. 'San Gimeno is not a primitive island,' she declared obliquely, avoiding his question. 'It's not commercialised, I admit, but that doesn't mean it lacks the necessary amenities.'

'I get the feeling you find our situation hard to handle,' he said softly, just as if she hadn't spoken. 'That's why you turned down my offer of the helicopter, is it not? It is also why you persuaded Mike Delano not to let me know what you were doing. Come on, Olivia, that's the truth, *no*?' He made a derisive sound. '*Dios*, what did you expect me to do? Jump your bones?'

Olivia had heard enough. She stood up. Ignoring him, she turned purposefully towards the door, but before she could reach it Christian's hand caught her arm.

'Wait!'

'Why should I?'

Yet Olivia knew better than to try and get away from him. His fingers were long and narrow, it was true, but they were also immensely strong. No amount

of useless struggle on her part would free her until he
was ready to let her go.

All the same, it was hard to remain still under his
searching appraisal. She was acutely aware that he
was breathing heavily now and she guessed her sudden dash for the door had caught him unawares. She
doubted he appreciated having to reason with her, either, and his expression mirrored the ambivalence he
felt.

Even so, when he spoke it was an apology. 'I
shouldn't have said that,' he said, his nostrils flaring
with the effort to control the anger that was riding
him. 'I'm sorry.'

'Are you?'

Her answer was hardly original, but in the circumstances it was impossible to think of anything unique.
Her treacherous senses were registering other things,
like his heat and his nearness, and the predatory mag-
netism that exuded from his pores.

He was a dangerous man, in more ways than one,
and his next words were just as disturbing. 'Of course
I am,' he said, the pad of his thumb abrading the inner
curve of her wrist. 'I do not want us to be enemies,
Olivia.'

His voice had thickened as he spoke, and once
again she heard the sensual accent he'd used that fate-
ful night. Her stomach quivered at the realisation that
he was playing with her. That he was using his not-
inconsiderable skills as an advocate in the effort to
make her change her mind. He was far cleverer than
she had given him credit for and her heart skipped a
beat.

Years ago, Tony had insisted on her accompanying
him to the courthouse in Miami to watch Christian

defend a case of industrial espionage that had been brought against the Mora Corporation. He'd won, of course, proving that the plaintiff's real aim had been to lower the company's value with the scam. Those were the skills he was using on her now, she thought breathlessly, combined with a subtle persuasion that was as seductive as it was counterfeit. He was determined to have his own way. Christian Rodrigues had no intention of changing his life to look after his cousin's son.

'I'm sure Luis must be back from the examination room now,' she said, refusing to look at him. It was enough that she was aware of him with every fibre of her being. She didn't need to see for herself what a gullible fool he thought she was.

'I don't think this is about Luis.' Christian's voice was flat now, but she didn't make the mistake of accepting his apparent disappointment at face value.

'I don't care what you think,' she declared, glancing significantly towards the door. Then she looked down at his hand gripping her wrist. For a moment the contrast between his much darker skin and her paler flesh arrested her, but she forced herself not to think of it. Then, fighting back the urge to lift her head, she added, 'Are you going to let me go, or am I going to have to scream for help?'

Christian made a sound of impatience. 'You wouldn't do that, *querida*,' he said, using the Spanish endearment deliberately, she was sure. His breath fanned the moist hollow between her breasts and she knew he was looking down at her. 'Think how embarrassing it would be for Luis if his stepmother and his cousin were found in—shall we say, compromising circumstances?'

Olivia's chin jutted. 'You think Luis would take your word for what happened over mine?'

'No.' Christian sighed. 'I'm just trying to make you see how ridiculous it is for us to quarrel. We both want what's best for Luis, don't we?'

'I do.'

'And I do, too.'

'So long as it doesn't interfere with your life.'

'Have I said so?'

'You didn't have to.' Olivia made a helpless gesture. 'You know how Luis would feel living at Bal Harbour with you.'

'Are you sure it is Luis you are thinking about?' he queried softly. 'Is it not nearer the truth to say that you don't want me living in *your* house?'

'It's not my house. It's Tony's.'

'But Tony is not here any more. And he left that house to you, Olivia.'

'And I don't want it.'

'Because of what happened there?'

'No!' She felt sick at the thought. But she had been at the house the night Tony died. A vivid image of her naked body, spread-eagled on the huge colonial bed in the master bedroom, with Christian straddling her, his tongue laving a burning path from her nipple to her navel, swept over her. 'I—I just don't want to live there,' she choked. Then, with slightly more control, 'It will always be Tony's house to me.'

'And what happened between us has no bearing on that decision?'

She shook her head. 'No.'

'You're a liar, Olivia.'

She managed a derisive snort. 'It takes one to know one.'

Christian waited a beat. 'So what are you saying?'

'I'm saying that Luis will—will expect me to be there for him,' she muttered unwillingly. 'And you've known that all along.' She blew out a breath. 'Now, please: just let me go.'

For a moment she thought he was going to ignore her request. But then, like a trap springing, he opened his fingers and stepped back from her. *'Muy bien,'* he said, spreading his hands. 'Far be it from me to keep a mother from the child she loves.'

She did look at him then, her eyes wide with indignation, and he moved his shoulders in a dismissive gesture. 'What?' he asked at her outraged stare, and she was tempted to tell him exactly what she thought of his shameless manipulation.

'Just—just keep away from me in future,' she said instead. And, hoping he hadn't noticed the tremor in her voice, she turned determinedly towards the door.

Luis was back in his room when she reached his door and pushed it open. He was lying on his back, as he had been before, his eyes the only part of his head that moved.

'Hi,' she said softly, trying to ignore the fact that Christian was behind her. 'Everything okay?'

'So they say,' Luis muttered wearily, his depression evident in the twist of his mouth. 'Where have you been? I was afraid you'd gone.'

'Your stepmother and I have been discussing what to do when you get out of here,' declared Christian, before Olivia could say anything. He stepped closer to the bed. 'I suggested opening up the house at Bal Harbour, but I'm not sure she will agree.'

Luis's brows drew together in confusion and Olivia gave Christian a furious look. How typical of him to pre-empt her decision. He knew that the best method of defence was attack.

Thinking on her feet, she said quickly, 'I haven't decided where we're going to stay yet.' She covered the young man's hand with her own. 'Wherever it is, we'll be together. Now—what did the doctor say?'

'The usual.' Luis clearly wasn't interested in medical matters. 'What did Christian mean about you opening up the Bal Harbour house? Aren't you living there?'

'Not right now, no.' Once again Olivia silently berated Christian for putting her in this position. 'I told you before you returned to college, didn't I? I said I wanted to get away on my own for a while. I've been staying on an island in the Bahamas. It's beautiful there this time of year, as you know.'

'I see.'

Luis absorbed this in sullen silence and Olivia knew she had to go on. She forced a smile. 'But, naturally, I don't have to stay there. You and I—we look out for each other, don't we?' She ignored Christian as she added, 'We're the only two Moras left.'

For now.

The thought sprang irresistibly into her mind. And depending on the speed of his recovery, she might have to tell Luis she was expecting a baby sooner rather than later. How would he react when he discovered her dilemma? Whatever, she had no desire to find out with Christian looking on.

'So what are you saying?' Luis asked at last. 'That you're willing to come home and look after me?' His mouth took on a sulky curve. 'Don't put yourself out.'

If I don't, who will? thought Olivia ruefully, once

again keeping it to herself. 'We'll work something out,' she said, wishing Christian would go. 'Maybe you could come and stay on San Gimeno with me.'

'No!'

Christian's denial was instantaneous and shocking. What the hell did it have to do with him? she brooded, giving him a challenging look. 'Why not?' she countered, keeping a smile in place for Luis's benefit. 'The villa is perfect for his recuperation.'

'But San Gimeno is not,' declared Christian flatly. 'Luis may need therapy; nursing. You're not suggesting the facilities on San Gimeno compare to those here?'

Olivia hadn't thought of that. But then, she'd hardly had time to give the matter serious consideration. He could be right. Luis might need expert attention. But it was the only solution she could think of to satisfy her needs as well.

Luis came unexpectedly to her assistance. 'I think that's a great idea,' he said, showing more enthusiasm than he'd shown thus far. There was a sudden glint of excitement in his eyes that definitely hadn't been there earlier. 'You've got a villa, yeah?' He waited for Olivia's tentative nod, and then continued eagerly, 'Why can't we hire a nurse if we need one? And a physiotherapist, too. I bet they have a hospital there. People on San Gimeno get sick, don't they?'

'It's not that simple, Luis,' began Christian heavily, but even Olivia could see he was fighting a losing battle. However different from his father he might be in temperament, when Luis got his teeth into something he stuck to it. And right now he was gazing at her, waiting for her support.

'I think it might work,' she murmured, aware that

Christian was furious with her answer. But surely he didn't expect her to support him? Not when only minutes before he'd been threatening her plans.

'So do I.' Luis's enthusiasm was gathering strength. 'You can arrange it all, can't you, Chris? Like Olivia, I'd appreciate the chance to get away before the media pack find out where I am.'

Olivia couldn't look at Christian now. After all, that had been his argument when she'd demurred about using the helicopter. And there was no doubt that Luis would be less accessible on San Gimeno. Not all reporters had the resources Christian had employed to find her.

Now the older man straightened his shoulders and regarded Luis with a frustrated gaze. 'We will see what Dr Hoffman has to say,' he said obliquely. 'Whatever happens, you will not be leaving the hospital for several days at least.'

'Why not?' Luis was petulant now. 'What are they going to do with me? I've got to wear this freaking collar for God knows how long. They're not going to be able to do much until I get it off.'

'I don't think that's entirely true, Luis,' put in Olivia gently, not wanting to come down on Christian's side, but unable to ignore the facts. 'They may want to ensure the fracture's mending. They won't want your muscles to stiffen up.'

Luis sighed. 'I still don't see why I can't be treated elsewhere,' he muttered belligerently. 'A couple of days here, maybe. I can cope with that. But surely by the beginning of next week, I'll be ready to leave?'

'We'll see,' said Christian flatly, and earned himself another resentful glare.

'Hey, you're not my dad, Chris,' exclaimed Luis resentfully. 'Correct me if I'm wrong, but doesn't Olivia have the final say?'

CHAPTER FOUR

CHRISTIAN stood at the rail of the ferry as it eased its way into the small harbour. At this hour of a Sunday morning, the yachts and other sailing craft that had moored in San Gimeno overnight were still at their berths and the ferry's arrival caused them to bob up and down in their slips.

The ferry, which also served as a supply vessel, was the only large craft in the harbour. As Olivia had no doubt approved, San Gimeno didn't generate a lot of visitors and, in consequence, the ferry's arrival was a major event.

But although the harbour master appeared and his assistant came to help with docking the ferry, it was all very casual, very laid-back. Christian had to tamp down his impatience at the leisurely way the men called to one another and the good-natured ribbing that followed when the hawser fell into the water and had to be hauled out again.

Yet it was his own fault that he'd chosen to use the ferry instead of the helicopter that had flown him to Nassau. He could easily have ordered his pilot to come back today and take him the comparatively short distance to San Gimeno. But he hadn't. He'd let the man think he was spending the whole four days in Nassau instead of admitting that he was primarily here to check on his cousin.

Of course, he'd managed to mix business with family matters. Before his death, Tony had been exploring the feasibility of opening a branch of the Mora Investment Company in the Bahamas, and this visit gave Christian the ideal opportunity to investigate further.

Which was just the sort of attitude Olivia abhorred, he acknowledged ruefully, his thin lips flattening against his teeth. She'd never liked him, never trusted him. Never understood how grateful he'd been to Tony for the chance he'd given him. It wasn't that she despised his ambition precisely. It was simply her belief that everything he did was to further his own ends.

Which wasn't true.

The ferry bumped against the jetty, the rubber siding squeaking its own protest, and Christian moved forward to disembark. He had no luggage as such. Just the inevitable briefcase that held a few personal items as well as the laptop computer he'd been working on. He supposed he was an odd visitor for the ferry to carry even if his loose-fitting cargo pants and black polo shirt were less formal than his usual attire. But, compared to the frayed shorts and sleeveless tees of his fellow passengers, he still looked different. Even if his skin was only marginally lighter than theirs.

Gaining the concrete landing, Christian looked about him. The quay itself was piled with crates of all kinds: shellfish, wedged into ice-filled boxes that leaked a steady stream of water onto the ground; sacks of okra and beans, and root vegetables; bananas turning yellow in the sun.

Christian turned his back on the ferry and started along the quay, only now realising that he'd made no provision for getting out to Olivia's villa. He knew it was on the south side of the island. Luis had told him that much when he'd spoken to him two days ago. But, without giving away his reasons, there'd been no way he could have asked for directions.

Above the harbour, the colour-washed roofs of the small town of San Gimeno dotted the hillside. The main street sloped up between shacks selling everything from baby clothes to diving gear. A small food market was just opening its doors and the smell of hot bacon and fried eggs was almost irresistible. But Christian had grabbed a coffee before they'd left Nassau, and he wasn't particularly hungry right now.

Was he nervous?

The idea infuriated him. He shouldn't be. He had every right to come and see Luis. He didn't need to ask anyone's permission. So why had he chosen to come on the morning ferry, instead of noisily announcing his arrival in the company chopper?

Because he hadn't wanted to attract attention, he told himself shortly. It had nothing to do with turning up unexpectedly and catching Olivia unawares. All right, so he knew she wouldn't be pleased to see him. Was it so terrible to want her to meet him unprepared?

But how the hell was he going to get out to the south shore? He hadn't seen any taxis and if there were any he doubted they'd be plying their trade at this hour of the morning. It was still only eight o'clock, and the island was barely stirring. Without the ferry's arrival, he doubted there'd have been anyone about.

Then, at the top of the street, where a road sign indicated that it was seven miles to Cocoa Beach, he saw a pick-up truck lumbering towards him. Flagging

it down, he explained his dilemma, and after a generous sum of dollars had changed hands the driver
agreed to drive him out to the south shore.

It was not a comfortable trip. The truck had no
suspension to speak of and its brakes were only marginally better. It only picked up speed on the straight
and was jammed into a lower gear for the corners.
This caused the vehicle to lurch wildly from side to
side and make Christian glad he hadn't succumbed to
the lure of the bacon.

But at least he was heading in the right direction.
He knew Olivia's address was in Cocoa Beach and
how many villas occupied by solitary white women
could there be? From Luis's description, he knew it
was near the ocean. Despite her desire to leave
Miami, Olivia obviously hadn't wanted to move far
from the sea.

His driver was a taciturn character. Once he'd got
Christian's money in his hand, he'd lapsed into a
moody silence. The only noise in the cab was the
radio, which was tuned to a station that only played
reggae and rap. Christian's head was throbbing by the
time they reached the other end of the island.

The small village where he got out couldn't be anywhere else but Cocoa Beach. With its whitewashed
cottages it was quiet and peaceful. A breeze blew off
the ocean, cooling his aching head and making him
aware of the beauty all around him. Long beaches
stretched out on either side of a stone-flagged jetty,
where water that was a dazzling blue-green in the
shallows turned to deepest cobalt further out.

The road here was just packed earth bleached to an
overall sand colour by the sun. Dwellings with closed
shutters presented blank faces to the street and only

a couple of children who were playing with a stray dog gave him an inquiring look as he walked by.

He couldn't immediately see any place that looked like the villa Luis had described to him. But he was loath to ask the children for directions. Instead, he looped the strap of his briefcase over his shoulder, and vaulted down onto the beach.

He walked along the shoreline, his expensive deck shoes leaving dark footprints in the damp sand. Beyond the village, trees clustered close to the dunes, palms and swamp cypress that did a good job of hiding any isolated dwellings from public view.

And then he saw her.

She was just coming out of the water and, although she was still some distance away, Christian knew instinctively that it was her. She had evidently been taking an early morning swim and as he watched she swept her hair back from her face with both hands.

Her hands lingered at her neck and he guessed she was completely unaware of how this action caused her breasts to push against the thin fabric that covered them. She was wearing one of those strappy cropped tops that these days were teamed with bikini briefs, and between the top and the skimpy briefs her midriff looked slim and brown and unexpectedly sexy. In fact, with her silvery hair darkened and slick against her head, every delicate line of her face and body was exposed in profile, long legs completing a picture of unknowingly sensual womanhood.

Dios!

Christian's fingers tightened around the strap of his briefcase and he was aware that his body had tightened, too. His trousers felt uncomfortably tight suddenly and he was forced to adjust them before continuing towards her.

He swore savagely to himself; he wasn't sexually attracted to Olivia. He couldn't be. He'd rationalised what had happened the night Tony died and at no time had he allowed himself to afford the incident anything more than impulse status. He'd delivered his devastating news and he'd comforted her. If he'd enjoyed it more than he should then perhaps that said more about her response than his.

Nevertheless, as he watched her bend to pick up the towel she had left on the sand his groin ached with sudden remembrance. It had been so good to bury his hard flesh in the moist cleft he'd found between her legs, so satisfying to feel her legs around him and the convulsive shudders of her climax that had overwhelmed his good sense.

It was the first time since he was a schoolboy that he'd had sex with a woman without first taking any precautions. These days such measures were automatic, but for once he'd broken his own code. Why? Because he knew for a fact that since she'd married Tony there'd been no other men? Or because there'd been no pregnancies, either?

But suddenly he knew that given the chance he'd do it again. The sweet curve of her bottom was undeniably appealing and as she straightened his palms itched to slide beneath the top of her swimsuit and find her rounded breasts.

Her hand went almost instinctively to the slight swell of her stomach and for a moment she looked almost pensive. Then her fingers inched the briefs a little lower and Christian's mouth dried. *Dios*, was she going to peel them off?

But no. After a moment, her hands went to the small of her back and she arched her spine. Evidently all she was doing was stretching after her swim and it was his fault if he was ascribing a sexual motivation to her movements. He'd been too long without a woman, he decided grimly. He had no interest in the frozen widow as Dolores had said.

He didn't know what made her notice him at that moment. Maybe something of the frustration he was feeling had reached out to her. However it happened, she saw him then, and for a moment something like panic crossed her face. Then, with a rapid movement she gathered up the towel and wrapped it about her shoulders, successfully hiding all but the long shapely legs from his evidently unwelcome gaze.

'What are you doing here?' she demanded, when it must have been perfectly obvious why he was here. And as he covered the remaining few yards between them, 'Where did you come from?'

'Well, I didn't materialise out of the ether,' he told her shortly, resenting the hostility with which she greeted his most innocent action. 'How do you think I got here? I took the ferry from Nassau. I, too, can be unpredictable.' He gave her a challenging stare. 'Okay?'

He could see that she wanted to say that it was not okay, that he should have warned her that he was coming, and that he had no right to turn up here unannounced. Her grey eyes flashed with a cold fire and he guessed that even now she couldn't look at him without remembering what he'd done. What *they'd* done, he amended grimly. He refused to take all the blame.

Even if right at this moment he was tempted to pull her down onto the sand and repeat the offence.

'Didn't Luis tell you I'd spoken to him a couple of nights ago?' Christian continued as she nudged her feet into backless sandals. He'd never realised bare feet could look so sexy, he thought irritably. Yet he was aware of everything about her, from the seawater that sparkled on her lashes to the white teeth that nibbled at her lower lip.

'He may have done,' she replied now, as if any news about him would have been of supreme indifference to her. Then, as if suddenly discovering another pitch, 'Are you alone?' She glanced over his shoulder as if looking for his companion. 'Didn't— who is it you're seeing at the moment? *Julie?* Did she come with you?'

He managed not to rise to the provocation. 'What are you saying?' he asked. 'That if I'd brought a girlfriend I'd have been welcome here?'

She cast him a look out of the corners of her eyes as she started across the sand that said what she thought of that response. But a gap in the trees revealed a sprawling villa, he saw now. Then, with a little shrug, she said softly, 'It would have been more in character, don't you think?'

Christian's jaw clamped on the words that struggled for expression. *Dios*, she had no right to say that to him. Who he saw and when was not her problem. But what annoyed him most was the knowledge that since Tony died—since he'd made love to *her*, in fact—he'd found it bloody impossible to get sexually aroused by anyone else.

'Perhaps I was afraid you might be jealous,' he taunted at last, deciding that if she felt she had the right to mock him he could do the same, and he heard her sudden intake of breath.

'Don't you—don't you dare say that to me,' she declared in a low, impassioned voice. 'I'm not one of your—conquests!'

He guessed that wasn't the epithet she'd like to have used but she was too much of a lady to sink to that level. Nevertheless, her self-control infuriated him and he responded without thinking.

'Hey, and I'm not your husband,' he mimicked, matching his stride to hers, and her face flamed with hot colour.

'Go to hell!' she retorted, quickening her step and she was ahead of him as they passed between the belt of palms and started up a grassy slope towards the house.

Christian didn't want to be impressed with the place but he was. A wraparound veranda, where bamboo chairs and tables provided a welcome retreat from the heat of the sun, opened into a coolly tiled hall. Rooms here expanded on either side: light, spacious apartments with lots of limed oak furniture and soft, squashy sofas. Cushions were scattered on chairs and sofas competing with the many flower arrangements for colour. It was elegant, yet warmly inviting, and he recognised Olivia's touch in the photographs of Luis and herself that decorated the mantel, and the flower prints that used to hang on the walls of the Miami apartment.

'Nice,' he said admiringly, but she didn't answer him. Instead, she turned to the dark-skinned woman of indeterminate age who had emerged from the back of the house.

'Susannah,' she said tersely. 'Would you give

Mr—er—Rodrigues whatever he wants, please? I want to go and get changed.'

'Not on my account, I hope,' murmured Christian wickedly, unable to resist the retort.

He didn't really understand why he got so much pleasure out of baiting her, but he did. Olivia gave him a savage glare before walking away, heading towards the rooms at the back of the villa.

In her room, Olivia took the first full breath she'd dared since she'd turned her head and seen Christian coming towards her along the beach.

God, to begin with she'd half believed she was imagining things. That the thoughts she'd had when she'd come out of the water and run her hands over the distinct swell of her abdomen had somehow conjured up his likeness out of thin air.

She'd been wondering what her baby would be like, who he—or she—would look like. For the first time she'd wondered what she'd do if it looked like its father. Thank goodness Luis's accident had happened in the early months of her pregnancy. Although she was over five months now, her natural slenderness meant that she could usually disguise the thickening contours of her waistline with loose shirts and flowing dresses.

Christian was not like her stepson, however. And when she'd realised he could see her, that he had probably watched her as she'd examined her stomach, she'd known real panic. Christian was a man, with a man's experience. Surely enough experience to know if a woman was pregnant or not.

She shuddered now as she dropped the towel and stripped off her swimsuit. She'd never dreamt he might turn up here uninvited, although now she berated herself for not thinking of it before. It was exactly the sort of thing Christian would do, just to disconcert her. And if he thought—

What? *What?*

As she stepped into the shower she remembered what he'd said when she'd taunted him about his women. He couldn't honestly believe that she was jealous but she would have to be careful what she said in future. She didn't want to come off sounding as if it mattered, that what *he* did concerned her. For heaven's sake, if she had a choice she'd never see him again.

But that wasn't going to happen. Although it was over a month since Luis's accident and four weeks since his doctors had agreed to him continuing his convalescence here, no one really knew how long it was going to take. It depended on how quickly Luis's pelvis healed and whether there were any complications. Until then, Olivia felt as if her own life had been put on hold.

Unfortunately, however, her pregnancy wouldn't be thwarted. She was already used to feeling the life stirring deep in her womb. In normal circumstances, she'd have been thrilled at this development. She *was* thrilled. Christian couldn't spoil that. But she was trapped, and it was hard not to feel uneasy at his arrival.

She stepped out of the shower and wrapped herself in one of the thick towels she'd brought from the apartment. She wished she had someone in whom she could confide. Susannah was kind, but she wouldn't understand Olivia's feelings. No, she had only herself to depend on and that was that.

Getting used to sharing the villa with Luis and his nurse hadn't been easy, either. Although there were four bedrooms, the reception rooms were limited, and she'd had to give up the room in which she'd planned to do her writing so that Luis's physiotherapist could have a room to work in. For a few days, Olivia had half wished she'd taken Christian's advice and opened up the house in Bal Harbour which was so much bigger. But then she'd squashed her moans and acknowledged that Luis seemed happier here.

And she had been happier, too, until Christian had turned up...

Dropping the towel, she caught a glimpse of herself in the bathroom mirror and paused to take a closer look. Did she really look pregnant? Was it obvious? Would anyone actually associate her thickening waistline with a baby if they didn't know?

She rather thought they might. Apart from anything else, her breasts were fuller, the nipples darker, distended by changes she didn't even want to consider. Oh, God, if only Christian had stayed away, she could have handled this. As it was she felt like Damocles under the sword.

Usually, she'd wear shorts and a loose shirt, but today she felt unwilling to expose herself to Christian's critical gaze. Instead she donned a strappy cotton sundress that was caught beneath her breasts by a satin ribbon. It was patterned in shades of pink and green and had always been one of her favourites. Christian might even recognise it. And if he did it might squash any suspicions he might be tempted to explore.

It was almost ten o'clock when she walked back into the living room. She had hoped that Christian might be sitting on the veranda, where she usually had her breakfast, but to her annoyance he was sprawled on one of the sofas talking to Helen Stevens, Luis's nurse. He got to his feet as soon as she appeared, but not before Olivia had had the chance to see them; to register the easy intimacy they apparently shared.

Of course, Christian had met Helen before. He'd insisted on arranging for Luis's private medical care himself. It was only now that it occurred to Olivia to wonder exactly how well he knew her. She disliked the thought that Nurse Stevens might be another of Christian's ex-girlfriends.

Helen stood up, too, as Olivia came in, her attitude flustered, as if aware that she'd been caught out in a less than professional situation. 'Luis is still asleep,' she said, her freckled features showing a trace of embarrassed colour. 'He had a bad night. Now that he's feeling stronger, the cast on his leg is beginning to chafe.'

'But he's all right otherwise?' Her own problems forgotten, Olivia gazed at the nurse with concerned eyes.

'Oh, yes.' Helen grimaced, pushing back her curly dark hair with a careless hand. 'He's impatient, that's all.' She glanced at Christian, her lips twitching into an attractive smile. 'I was just telling Mr Rodrigues, he can't wait to get into the sea. I don't blame him. Looking out on all that blue water every day and not being able to enjoy it must be torture!'

Olivia's lips tightened. 'Are you suggesting he would have been happier convalescing elsewhere?'

'I—no—'

Helen looked uncomfortable now and, as if taking

pity on her, Christian intervened. 'I think what Nurse Stevens is saying is that Luis's surroundings are encouraging him in his recovery,' he remarked mildly. 'I for one am delighted to hear that he's eager to get better.'

The heat poured into Olivia's throat. He spoke as if she weren't delighted, too. But then, he was only intent on humouring the other woman. In presenting himself in the most attractive light.

Whatever, she resented it, and as soon as Nurse Stevens had excused herself and left the room she drew a steadying breath. 'I hope Susannah provided you with everything you needed,' she remarked tersely. 'You seem to have made a conquest of one of my staff at least.'

Christian's lips twisted. 'Not nearly.'

'Perhaps I was mistaken.' But Olivia knew she didn't sound as if she thought she was. 'Did she find time to fill you in on Luis's progress?' she added coolly. 'Or were you too busy reminiscing about old times?'

His dark eyes narrowed with amusement. 'Careful, Olivia, I may begin to think you are jealous, after all.'

Olivia gasped. 'You should be ashamed to say such a thing to me.'

'Ashamed?' His eyes darkened. 'That's a strange word to use in the circumstances. Do you want to explain exactly what you mean?'

'If you need me to tell you—'

'Ah, right. We are back to what occurred the night Tony died.' He shook his head. 'I had hoped we had got past that. I wish you'd put it completely out of your mind.'

'I wish, too,' exclaimed Olivia fiercely, and then

swallowed convulsively as a look of bafflement crossed his lean dark face.

'What do you mean?' He stared at her.

'Forget it.'

Olivia turned away, aware that she had spoken recklessly again. Dear God, if she wasn't careful he was going to guess that something was bothering her. And not just the fact that he'd come here unannounced.

His breath suddenly moistened the taut curve of her nape, and she realised he had come to stand behind her. It took all of her will-power not to try and step away. 'It is you who seems to be having a problem, Olivia, *querida*,' he murmured softly. He blew on her neck. 'I have to ask myself why.'

'I...' She was lost for words. She had the craziest impulse to press her hands to her stomach and feel the reassuring tremor of the life within her. But that was something she couldn't do, not in his presence, and, expelling an uneven breath, she added, 'I suppose it's because I never—cheated on my husband before.'

Christian stifled an oath. 'Strictly speaking you didn't cheat on your husband,' he said roughly, and as if he needed some reassurance, too, his hands closed about the narrow bones of her shoulders. 'Dammit, Olivia, stop beating yourself up over something we can't alter. Tony's dead. He was dead when—well, you know when. I don't have to spell it out for you. You have nothing to blame yourself for.'

Don't I?

Olivia quivered, aware that his hands on her shoulders were far too real, far too appealing. This was her cue to tell him what she thought of him for dismissing what had happened so casually, but instead of that she was imagining how delightful it would be to lean against his tall frame. To let his hard body take the strain. Tony had said, times out of number, how much Christian could be relied upon. Unfortunately, she couldn't allow herself to feel the same.

'So who do I blame?' she asked, forcing herself to move away from him now. 'You?'

Christian's lean face hardened. 'If that's what it takes to get you over this, why not?' he replied wearily. 'In any case, I didn't come here to fight with you, *mi amor*. I just wanted to see my cousin. Surely that is not a crime even with you.'

Olivia took a deep breath. 'Okay.' She refused to respond to his deliberate endearment and composing her features, she turned to face him again. 'So—how long are you planning to stay?'

CHAPTER FIVE

LUIS was on the veranda when Christian got back from town.

Parking the open-topped Jeep he'd leased from a dealer in San Gimeno at the side of the villa, Christian swung out of the cab. Then, reaching in again, he collected the bag containing the shorts and tee shirts he'd bought in town, before striding across the grass to the veranda steps.

In recent days, Luis had spent more and more time outdoors, and his skin was gradually losing the unhealthy pallor it had worn since his accident. He looked infinitely more cheerful, too, as if he was beginning to see a light at the end of his particular tunnel.

'Hi,' he said now as Christian mounted the steps. He didn't have to wear the cervical collar any more, and he nodded towards the Jeep. 'You've got some wheels.'

'Well, I didn't like the idea that your stepmother has to rely on taxis to get about,' said Christian easily, already aware that Olivia probably wouldn't thank him for it. 'What do you think?'

Luis's mouth tilted at the corners. 'Well, I wouldn't have said that shade of pink was your colour,' he teased. 'But what do I know?'

'Yeah.' Christian acknowledged his comment with a wry grimace. 'But it'll get you about. You may be glad of it one day.'

'You mean you'll allow me to drive it?' Luis patted his chest with a mocking hand. 'Be still my beating heart!'

Christian pulled a face. 'You can mock, but you're hardly in a position to argue.' He arched a brow. 'So how are you feeling? I see they've supplied you with crutches to get around.'

Luis scowled. 'I don't think anyone realises how awkward it is getting out of a chair in the first place. Why can't I just sit here until the bone heals itself?'

'You know why not.' Christian sympathised, but he tried to speak positively. 'You've got to get some exercise. Have they offered you some weights?'

'I'm not into muscle-building,' muttered Luis sulkily. But then, as if realising he was being mean-spirited, he changed his tack. 'What about you? How long are you staying here? Mom says you haven't told her what your plans are.'

Did she? Christian hesitated and then dropped down onto one of the bamboo loungers. Facing Luis, he set down his bag and then rested his arms along his spread thighs. 'I haven't decided,' he declared, with a shrug of his broad shoulders. 'I'll let you know when I do.'

'Hey, it's not my villa,' said Luis carelessly. 'It's Mom you have to please.'

'What's that supposed to mean?' Christian's brows drew together. 'What has your stepmother said?'

'I guess you'd know that better than me,' responded Luis with a wry expression on his face. 'What's with you and her anyway? I may be a physical wreck, but my brain's still working. I'd have to be blind not to see the sparks you two strike off one another.'

Christian turned his head abruptly and gazed towards the ocean. 'You're imagining things.'

'Am I?' Luis snorted. 'Come on, Chris. You hate one another's guts. You know you do. Why don't you admit it? You don't like it when she calls the shots.'

'That's not true.' Christian had himself in control again and he gave his cousin a warning stare. Then, rubbing his palms over the knees of his khaki trousers, he added shortly, 'Olivia and I hardly know one another.'

'Yeah, right.'

Patently, Luis didn't believe him and Christian was irritated at the way the boy's words had hit a nerve. Were he and Olivia so transparent? He had thought he had done a reasonably good job of hiding his feelings, particularly in the face of Olivia's provocation. But evidently he'd been wrong.

Pushing himself up from the lounger, he forced a thin smile. 'We must agree to differ, *mi amigo*,' he said, knowing that he ought to have been able to laugh it off. He glanced into the villa. 'Do you need anything? Can I get you something before I go and change?'

'Like what?' Luis was sardonic. 'A woman?' He grimaced. 'Do you know how long it's been since I got laid?'

'It's not something I've spent sleepless nights over, no,' retorted Christian drily. 'What I meant was, do you want a drink? It's pretty hot out here.'

'Isn't it though?' Luis flexed his back wearily. Then, as if acknowledging that he was being a pain, he gave a rueful grin. 'No, I'm okay. The physio will be here shortly. And I don't like to drink too much before he comes or I get an uncomfortable need to take a leak while he's doing his stuff.'

'That could be a problem,' agreed Christian, feeling his tension returning at the prospect of seeing Olivia again. 'So where's your mother? I'd better tell her I'd like to stay on.'

'She's around here somewhere.' Luis reached for a magazine that was lying on the table beside him. 'I think she's under the impression that you've already left.'

Yeah. Christian didn't say so, but he conceded the boy's point as he went to deposit his purchases in his room. He hadn't seen Olivia before he went to town and she might not have noticed he'd left his briefcase behind. But, what the hell? Surely she knew he'd tell her when he was leaving the island.

Now Christian flung the plastic bag on his bed and stood for a few moments breathing deeply. He still didn't truly understand what was making him act this way. Or, indeed, why he'd come to the island in the first place. Luis wasn't in any mortal danger; his injuries weren't life threatening in any way, and another phone call would have done just as well.

Okay, so saying he'd wanted to see the boy for himself wasn't exactly lying. Although he and Luis had hardly been close friends, they were family. But he had to ask himself whether, if Luis had still been at college in San Francisco, he'd have trekked across the country to check up on him. If he was honest would he admit that he'd wanted to see Olivia again?

Perhaps it was time he rang his office in Miami and found out what was happening at the Mora Corporation in his absence. Calling Mike Delano would certainly help him put things in perspective. Just for a moment there, Luis had scraped a nerve, and he didn't like it.

Olivia was coming back from a walk along the beach when she saw the pink Jeep turn up the drive towards the villa. She thought at first it must be Luis's therapist, who usually rode a scooter. But then she saw Christian emerge from the vehicle and her step slowed automatically. Dammit, what was Christian doing driving a Jeep? How long was he planning to stay?

When she'd been obliged to offer him a bed last night, she hadn't expected him to take that as an invitation to stay indefinitely. Okay, Luis had been pleased to see him, but her stepson would have been pleased to see anyone in his present condition.

Yet that wasn't entirely fair, she conceded grudgingly. Luis liked Christian. He admired him. It was probably only her imagination that made her think Luis was turning more to Christian now because Tony was dead. Whatever, the man had evidently expected to stay the night and Olivia had swallowed her resentment and had Susannah make up one of the spare beds. It was what Luis had expected and she couldn't disappoint her stepson.

Now, however, she regretted her generosity. Sheltering behind a palm tree, she thought how foolish she'd been in thinking they'd seen the last of him. When Susannah had told her he'd hired a cab to whisk him away to San Gimeno, she'd half believed he'd planned on catching the morning ferry. How wrong she'd been. Now it appeared he was settling in for a prolonged stay.

Sliding down against the tree, she tipped her head

back against the rough bark. She'd wait until Christian went indoors, she decided, viewing her bare knees with some regret. She should have worn a dress to go walking, not this thin shell and the silk shorts that barely covered her backside. Her *fat* backside, she emphasised glumly. Goodness knew, she was putting on weight.

Drawing up her knees, she let her arms fall disconsolately between her legs, digging her nails into the soft sand. The faint tremor below her ribcage reminded her that she had another hospital appointment in two days and she hoped Christian would be gone by then. Not just off the veranda, but off the island, she thought grimly. The last thing she needed was for him to offer to drive her into town.

Why, yes, she mouthed, inventing an imaginary conversation. *That's very kind of you, Christian. Yes, I have to see the gynaecologist. What? Oh, didn't I tell you I was pregnant? I'm going for another scan. I should have had it a couple of weeks ago, but what with Luis's accident and everything I missed my appointment. It doesn't do, you know, to neglect these things.*

Her jaw bunched, and she lifted her hands and swept the lingering grains of sand from her fingers. Well, there was no point in speculating about it because that conversation wasn't going to happen. This was her baby, not his. And if, just occasionally, she felt a twinge of contrition about deceiving him, she had only to think about how he had behaved since it had happened to justify her decision.

Turning her head, she looked back towards the veranda and saw that Christian was sitting down now. Dammit, she thought, how long was he going to stay there? She needed the loo, another result of her pregnancy. If she could only hear what they were saying she might have had a better idea how long their conversation was going to last.

Still, she was surprised when Christian suddenly got to his feet again. It seemed rather sudden. Was it something Luis had said? Maybe they'd had an argument, she mused, without much optimism. Christian was far too clever an operator to risk losing his cousin's support.

Whatever, he picked up the bag he'd been carrying earlier and after another brief exchange with Luis he strode into the villa. But he didn't act as if he had any doubts about his destination. He was probably going to have a shower to cool down.

Great!

Olivia sighed and, after waiting a few moments to make sure he hadn't just gone to fetch something from his room, she pushed herself stiffly to her feet. Her shorts were flecked with sand and she brushed at them energetically. It wouldn't do for Luis to start speculating that she was avoiding their unexpected guest.

She was barefoot and as she picked her way up the sloping lawn to the villa she thought how dramatically things had changed in the past four weeks. She'd almost forgotten the freedom she'd experienced in the weeks before Luis's accident. Now, the threads of her old life were wrapped securely about her again.

Luis gave her a sardonic look as she came up onto the veranda. 'Had a nice walk?' he asked, laying aside the magazine he'd picked up after Christian's departure, and Olivia forced a bright smile.

'I've had a lovely walk,' she said firmly, resisting

the urge to put her hands on her hips and flex her aching back. 'How are you feeling?'

'I'm fine.' Luis regarded her critically. 'But perhaps you'd like to tell me what you were doing hiding behind that palm tree down there?'

Olivia's lips parted in dismay. 'I—I wasn't hiding.'

'No?' Luis was sceptical. 'So what were you doing? Taking a rest before scaling the north face of the south lawn?'

Olivia's mouth compressed. 'I—I was in no hurry to get back, that's all.'

'Because Chris was here.'

She shrugged. 'Maybe.' She smoothed the pale blue shell over the waistband of her shorts and then, realising it outlined her stomach, as quickly released it again. 'Did he tell you how long he plans to stay?'

'The question of the hour.' Luis grimaced. 'No, he didn't. Why don't you ask him? I'm sure he'd be happy to discuss it with you.'

Olivia blew out a breath. 'You mean you asked him?'

'Wasn't I supposed to?'

'What you ask or don't ask has nothing to do with me,' she replied tartly. Then, realising she was inviting his derision, she added, 'Why has he hired that Jeep?'

'He says it's because we need some transport,' declared her stepson, his eyes moving past her to the garishly coloured vehicle parked beside the house. 'I guess he didn't have a lot to choose from. Somehow I don't think pink is Chris's colour of choice.'

Nor did Olivia, but she was still unhappy that he should have chosen to hire a motor vehicle in the first place. It smacked of permanency. Why couldn't he have used the island's taxi service like everyone else?

'You don't like Chris, do you?'

Luis's remark came out of left field and for a moment Olivia could only stare at him, not knowing what she was going to say.

Then, gathering herself, she said with what she hoped sounded like incredulity, 'I don't know where you've got that idea from. I hardly know the man.'

Luis gave her a retiring look. 'Come on, Mom. This is me you're talking to, not Dad. I've seen the way you look at Christian. Like you wished he'd take a hike off the nearest pier.'

Olivia was horrified. 'That's not true.'

'Sure it is.' Luis's breath hissed out on a long sigh. 'Like—what has he ever done to you?'

That was a little too close for comfort and Olivia felt her cheeks begin to burn. 'He's—he's done nothing to me,' she lied, pressing her damp palms into the small of her back anyway. 'I think you're getting fanciful, Luis. It's all this inactivity. It's having a negative effect on your brain.'

'You think?' Luis's brows drew together and she quickly dropped her arms to her sides. Then he frowned. 'Hey, you're not hung up on him, are you, Mom?' he exclaimed as if aware of her panic. 'Cos, I have to tell you honestly, you're not his type.'

'And he's not mine,' Olivia retorted swiftly, deciding she had had enough of this one-sided interrogation. 'Excuse me. I need the bathroom.'

'So why are you avoiding him?' Luis persisted as she crossed the veranda and, although she would have preferred to ignore him, caution advised her not to do anything to arouse his suspicions.

'I'm not avoiding him,' she exclaimed hotly, and then almost groaned aloud when the object of their discussion appeared at the sliding glass doors that opened onto the veranda. 'See,' she added, forcing a smile. 'Here he is now.'

Christian seemed to hesitate for a moment when he saw Olivia and she wondered briefly if he would have preferred to avoid her, too. He'd changed his clothes, she noticed. Instead of the khaki cargo pants he'd been wearing on his arrival, he was now sporting a pair of navy shorts that hung low on his narrow hips. A white sleeveless tank-top, which he hadn't bothered trying to tuck into his waistband, exposed a tantalising wedge of olive skin.

Luis evidently viewed Christian's reappearance as a bonus. Olivia guessed he was enjoying the hostility that he'd somehow sensed there was between them. In consequence, her tone was friendlier towards the older man than it might have been, and she said, with polite inquiry, 'Good morning. Did you sleep well?'

Christian's mouth flattened. He was probably remembering how incommunicative she had been last night at supper and speculating about her change of tone. But, dammit, she couldn't go on behaving as if he was the enemy. It would be much easier if she could act naturally and not go looking for trouble.

'I slept—very well,' he replied after a moment, but Olivia suspected that wasn't entirely the truth. His eyes looked deeper set than usual, and there were dark rings around them. Although the faintly haggard look suited him, it was not an indication that he was any easier with the situation than she was.

So why the hell didn't he just go?

But, 'Good,' she said, edging round him as he came

out onto the veranda. 'Now, if you'll both excuse me…'

'You're not leaving us, are you, Mom?'

Luis's face was full of devilment. Olivia told herself she was pleased that he was recovering his sense of humour, but she didn't appreciate him finding it at her expense.

'I'm sure you and—Christian have plenty to talk about,' she declared brightly. 'Besides, Jules will be here soon and I know he won't want me getting in his way.'

'So take Chris for a walk,' said Luis irrepressibly. 'I'm sure you don't want to neglect our guest.'

'I think your stepmother has better things to do than entertain me,' put in Christian, before she could say anything, and Olivia gave her stepson a warning look.

'That's right—' she began, only to break off as Christian interrupted her.

'In any case,' he added, proving he hadn't finished what he was saying, 'I was thinking of taking a swim. I doubt if Olivia wants to join me. She looks hot enough as it is.'

Olivia's lips pursed. She couldn't decide whether he was being sarcastic or not. Whatever, she resented the implication that the heat upset her. If he only knew, she thought dourly. It was him, and not the weather, that was heating her blood.

She couldn't help a prickle of awareness at the thought of seeing him in the water, however. She'd seen him naked before, of course, and despite everything the memory hadn't faded at all. Which was stupid when she considered how she felt about that occasion. Nonetheless, she knew Christian looked just as good without his clothes as he did with them on.

'I was just going for a shower,' she said, avoiding making any comment. 'If you'll excuse me, I'll see you both later on.'

'Shame,' observed Luis, unwilling to be robbed of his victory. 'Do you know, Chris, I think this is the first day Mom hasn't had a swim?'

Olivia blew out a breath. 'I probably will have a swim,' she said shortly. 'But later. When it's not so hot, as—as Christian says.' She forced a smile. 'Why don't you concentrate on those exercises you're supposed to have mastered, Luis? Instead of trying to cause trouble between your cousin and me.'

'Was that what I was trying to do?'

Luis widened his eyes innocently, and Olivia knew that if he'd been younger she'd have administered a severe rebuke. But with Christian looking on she was obliged to keep her temper, and pulling a face instead, she passed through the open window into the house.

In her room, however, her confidence deserted her. Sinking down onto the wide seat beneath the windows, she expelled a long breath. She didn't know which was worst, having Luis think she hated Christian or believing she was hung up on the man.

A movement beyond the windows caught her eye and she was glad of the distraction. A tall dark man was striding across the lawn in the direction of the beach. It was Christian, of course, and as she watched he pulled the vest he'd been wearing over his head.

His shorts hung low on his waist exposing the narrow bones of his hips and when his hands slipped into his waistband at his back she caught an involuntary breath. Surely he wasn't going to strip off, she thought incredulously. Not in sight of the windows. Okay, the beach was deserted, but surely common decency demanded he show his surroundings some respect?

When he glanced back at the villa she recoiled instantly. Could he see her? Did he suspect she was not taking the shower for which she'd made such a hasty retreat? But, no. With a cluck of impatience, she chided herself for even thinking she was visible. With the sun shining on the windows, there was no way she could be seen.

Nevertheless, she felt like a voyeur. Getting to her feet, she prepared to move away. But before she did she couldn't resist taking one last look out of the window, and her breathing quickened at the sight of Christian at the water's edge.

As she watched in disbelief he shucked off his shorts and dropped them on the sand behind him. The paler skin of his buttocks was clearly visible before he plunged into the sea. She let out an unsteady gasp. How dared he do that? *How dared he?* Her indignation soared. Just where the hell did he think he was?

In the shower, however, common sense reasserted itself. She was being silly. Seeing a naked man was nothing new to her. If he chose to swim in the nude, so what? He wasn't hurting anyone. Luis would probably do the same, given the chance.

The fact remained that Christian was not Luis. However she tried to rationalise her feelings, she couldn't regard him in the same light. He was nothing like Tony, either. When she looked at Christian's powerful body, she was instantly aware of how physically attractive he was.

And of how he had made her feel…

She shivered suddenly. Did he know that? Had he
chosen to strip off his clothes in plain sight of her
windows because he knew how susceptible she was?
If so, why had he done it? She didn't kid herself that
he might feel any lingering attraction towards her.

Until that night—and she didn't have to designate
which night—he'd never so much as looked at her.
Well, he had, but not with any attraction in mind.
There'd been times when she'd been sure he'd resented her presence. Maybe he believed she'd only
married Tony for his money. If so, he probably wasn't
alone.

Besides, the women Christian dated were all young
and beautiful. Julie, his present girlfriend, was just
another female who appeared to think he could do
no wrong. Tony used to joke about them, saying
Christian's girlfriends would always come second to
his ambition. And she believed it. That was why Tony
had relied on him so much.

Which brought her back to her own situation. She
sighed. Christian probably regretted what had happened just as much as she did. Well, maybe not quite
as much, she conceded, smoothing soap over the
rounding curve of her belly. Their brief intimacy had
had a lasting consequence. Because of that, it could
never be consigned to the past.

Of course, she could have had a termination. But
however she felt about her baby's father, that was
something she would never have done. She'd wanted
a child of her own for so long and she wanted this
baby desperately. She must not allow Christian's involvement to blind her to the way she felt.

Which reminded her again of her appointment at
the hospital in San Gimeno. Once she'd had this scan,

she wouldn't have to see the doctor again for a couple of weeks. She didn't want to put it off because of Christian. If only he would go back to Miami and leave her in peace.

CHAPTER SIX

HELEN STEVENS joined them for lunch, which made things easier. Although she didn't have a lot to say, she was a buffer between Christian and Olivia. He knew Olivia didn't want him here, but for some reason he was loath to give in to her unvoiced demands and leave. He hated to admit it, but the longer he spent with her, the more she intrigued him, and he deserved a break just as much as anyone else.

Besides, Mike Delano was doing a good job in his absence. The other man was obviously appreciating the chance to prove what he could do. While Tony was alive, he'd been unwilling to delegate authority to anyone but Christian. And as he and Mike kept in touch by phone and email, Christian was in no hurry to get back to work.

Which surprised him, he conceded, lifting his wineglass and taking a studied look at Olivia over the rim. It would have surprised her, too, if she'd known how he was feeling, he reflected. She was of the mistaken belief that work ruled his life.

Luis was enjoying himself, too, he noticed. The younger man was not averse to flirting with his nurse when he wasn't baiting either Christian or his stepmother. Christian wondered if Olivia knew that her stepson believed they disliked one another. The irony of that belief was not lost on him, particularly as Olivia probably agreed with Luis.

During the afternoon, Christian retired to his room

and spent some time working on his computer. Then he stretched out on his bed in the hope that he could catch up on some of the sleep he'd lost the night before. Whatever Olivia thought, he hadn't taken her hospitality for granted. And, although she'd offered him a bed for the night, he knew it was more for Luis's sake than his.

Consequently, he'd spent at least part of the night pondering the reasons why he'd come here. And, indeed, why he'd chosen to stay. The latter had something to do with the way he'd felt when he'd seen Olivia coming out of the water. Crazy as it surely was, he wanted to examine those feelings in more depth.

It amused him that she so transparently resented his friendship with Helen Stevens. He didn't really believe that she was jealous. She was just territorial, that was all. Like a cat, he mused, objecting to anyone who sank their claws into what she considered her possession. Yet she regarded him as the enemy despite the intimacy they had shared.

And that bugged him. Okay, maybe at one time she'd had some reason to suspect his motives for coming to work for Tony. He'd been a virtual stranger, after all, and Tony had taken him on trust. But since then he'd proved his loyalty a dozen times over. He'd had plenty of opportunities to betray his position if that was what he'd wanted to do.

And, until the night Tony had died, his contact with his cousin's wife had been brief. She'd spent most of her time in Bal Harbour, and, when she was in Miami, she'd rarely visited the Mora Building.

Christian knew her history, of course. Tony had told him how, when the aunt who had brought her up

had died, she'd answered his advertisement for a
nanny for Luis. Tony had had a thing about English
nannies and, after meeting Olivia for the first time,
Christian had understood why. She'd always appeared
to him to be calm and capable, and there was no doubt
that Luis depended on her a lot.

He hadn't known if that was why Tony had married
her. Knowing his cousin, he could quite believe that
Tony had been attracted to the young Englishwoman
and maybe she'd made marriage a condition of their
relationship. Whatever, by the time Christian had
come on the scene, Tony's ardour had cooled considerably. But that hadn't stopped him from warning the
younger man not to regard his wife as easy game.

And, until the night Tony had died, Christian had
never thought of her in that way...

The news that Tony was dead reached Christian at
eleven o'clock.

He'd spent most of the evening at the office, re-
searching a preliminary study concerning the shortfall
of oil revenues from their Pacific Rim operation. He'd
already had to field at least half a dozen complaining
calls from his girlfriend and when he'd got back to
his apartment and found his answering machine blink-
ing he'd been tempted to ignore it.

He hadn't, fortunately. The call, which had been
logged at ten forty-five, had been from Tony's latest
conquest. In panicked tones, the senator's wife had
been screaming for his help.

'He's dead!' Vicki Sutcliffe's voice was almost
unrecognisable. 'Hell, Rodrigues, where are you?
Tony's dead, have you got that? God Almighty, what
am I going to do?'

Christian thought later that it was a sign of her desperation that she'd rung him instead of the emergency services. As a politician's wife she'd learned to be very careful about what she said—and to whom. But right then he was too stunned to consider anything but the shocking news she'd delivered. When the call was disconnected, he continued to stare at the machine in disbelief.

His first impulse was to get back into his car and drive across town to Tony's apartment. It wasn't the apartment he shared with his wife. Ostensibly, it was kept for entertaining business clients only. But in all the years Christian had known his cousin, the only clients Tony had entertained there had been female. It was an unspoken belief in the office that the only person Tony was fooling was himself.

Now, however, he blew out a breath. Although he was desperate to see Tony for himself, to ensure that Vicki hadn't made a mistake, he hesitated. It was only fifteen minutes since she'd made the call. Snatching up the phone, he dialled the apartment.

And got the engaged signal.

Damn!

Cursing, he left his apartment and took the lift down to the basement garage. Although he guessed he was in a state of shock, he couldn't think about himself right now. Tony needed him. Whatever Vicki had said, it was Tony who mattered. He felt the unfamiliar prick of tears behind his eyes. Dammit, Tony couldn't be dead.

But he was. One look at Tony's body, sprawled obscenely across the big bed, confirmed his worst fears. He'd died, probably pursuing the excitement he'd striven all his life for. Christian's heart ached.

God alone knew how Tony's wife would cope with this.

There was no sign of Vicki in the apartment. She had evidently realised how precarious her position was. Nevertheless, her screams had attracted a crowd of onlookers from the other apartments and Christian had had to force his way through them to reach the door.

The police were already there, too. Someone, one of Tony's neighbours, no doubt, had called 911 as soon as they'd heard Vicki's screams. This was a genteel neighbourhood and they weren't used to witnessing such a scene.

It just got worse. The medical examiner was of the opinion that drugs were involved and his preliminary conclusion was that Tony's heart hadn't been up to the strain.

When the detective in charge of the investigation asked for the name of Tony's next of kin, Christian was devastated. This would annihilate Olivia, he thought, imagining how she would feel when she got the news. That was why he asked the officer if he could break the news to her. He couldn't let some nameless official crucify her like that.

'Just make sure she understands we'll need to take a statement from her,' the detective advised him flatly. 'We'll want statements from everyone, including yourself.' He paused. 'And Mr Mora's lady friend,' he added, with a rueful glance back into the bedroom. 'But that can wait until tomorrow morning. I doubt if we'll be accusing anyone at this stage.'

Not at any stage, Christian thought bitterly, if Senator Sutcliffe had anything to do with it. Whether he'd known what his wife was doing or not, he'd do everything in his power to hush this up. Which would suit him, too, Christian reflected. And Olivia. The media would have a field-day as it was.

An hour later, he stood in the spacious living room of Tony's Bal Harbour mansion. Only, strictly speaking, it wasn't Tony's mansion any more. The incredibility of that statement was still mind-blowing. Dammit, he had to be strong here. Tony would expect it of him. But the idea of facing a woman, who had never made any secret of her dislike of him, with news like this, was enough to freeze his blood.

Through the windows of the lamp-lit room, he could see the patio and the darkness of the ocean beyond it. The butler, who had admitted him a few moments ago, had switched on the floodlights before going in search of his mistress. It was an oasis of calm in a world gone mad, Christian thought, hardly able to believe that just a couple of hours ago he'd been anticipating his bed with some enthusiasm. The way he felt now, he doubted he'd ever sleep again.

Christian pushed his hands deep into the pockets of his jacket. The butler—Donelli—must have wondered what he was doing here when he opened the gates. But with his usual diplomacy, he'd said nothing, behaving as if admitting visitors at one in the morning were commonplace.

There were tubs of fuchsia and hibiscus on the patio. Their blossoms bloomed in the artificial light, spilling their bounty across the Italian tile. Scarlet and white. Like blood, he thought, quickly dismissing the comparison. Then, hearing a sound, he turned to find Olivia standing in the doorway behind him, watching him.

Her face was pale, and there was such a look of

fearful expectancy on it that he half suspected she knew why he was here. But she didn't. She couldn't. She was merely anxious, as any woman would be in the circumstances. It was a pity that Luis was away at college in California. Her sudden vulnerability tore his heart.

'Christian.' For once she used his given name. Generally she avoided addressing him at all. A pink tongue circled her upper lip. 'Is something wrong?'

Christian didn't know where to begin. Did she know about Tony's women? Did she care? Or course, she must. She was his wife—or, no, his widow. Oh, God, he wished he could save her from all this.

'Is—is it Luis?' Her voice was barely audible and he shook his head. It was significant that she had asked about her stepson first. She hesitated. 'Then it must be Tony,' she said, and he cursed himself anew for his inadequacy. 'What's happened? Has there been an accident? Is he badly hurt?'

'I'm sorry.' The words stuck in Christian's throat but he had to say them. He watched her as she weathered his words, wrapping the folds of her pale green silk robe about her like a shield. He suspected the robe was all she was wearing. He gathered himself grimly. 'I'm sorry, Olivia. Tony's dead.'

He saw her wince, saw the way she seemed to shrink in upon herself, pitied the stark disbelief in her gaze. She was trying desperately not to cry, which surprised him. Her pale face and twisting hands mirrored his own consternation when he'd heard Vicki Sutcliffe's words.

She swallowed then, a hand lifting automatically to her throat, bare above the cleavage of her robe. She wasn't wearing any jewellery, he noticed, not even her wedding ring. Her slender fingers were bare, her nails short and buffed with a pearlised gloss.

Her skin was clear of any make-up, thick lashes shading eyes of a particularly subtle shade of grey. Her hair, which he was used to seeing confined, flowed loose about her shoulders. Silvery-gold strands framed a face that looked as innocent as it was pure.

His gaze barely skimmed the rest of her, but he was sharply aware of his own reaction to her. He hadn't realised how tall she was before, or how high and round her breasts were. Her feet, bare beneath the hem of her robe, fascinated him in spite of himself.

He knew it was crazy. Tony was dead, for God's sake. This was not the time to be having intimate thoughts about his wife. Yet she was so different from the women he usually dated. Toothpicks, Tony used to call them. Not a real woman like this, warm and feminine, and incredibly sexy.

He stopped himself right there, appalled at the direction his thoughts had taken. But he realised now that he had always admired her, despite the hostility between them. It couldn't have been easy being married to a man who virtually ignored your existence. Yet, through it all she'd remained loyal. A better mother to Luis than Tony deserved.

All these thoughts passed through his head as he stood there feeling useless for the first time in his life. He'd always prided himself on his cool-headedness, his ability to handle any situation whatever the circumstances. But right now he felt helpless, impotent even, and it wasn't a good feeling.

'How—how did it happen?'

The question he'd been dreading broke into his abstraction and he struggled to formulate a reply. It was natural she would want answers and feeling sorry for himself wasn't going to help either of them. If he didn't tell her the truth, the police would. And without sparing the facts.

'He—the police think he may have had a heart attack,' he said, introducing the authorities' involvement deliberately. 'If it's any consolation, he probably knew very little about it.'

'The police?' As he'd expected she focussed on that. She shook her head a little bewilderedly. 'So it was an accident?'

'No.' Christian wished there were some way he could make this easier for her. 'It wasn't an accident. Tony was at—his apartment.'

A twinge of some emotion he couldn't recognise crossed her face as he spoke. Then her brow furrowed and her lips flattened tensely. 'He wasn't alone, was he?' she murmured. 'He was with another woman. I suppose you mean the Coconut Grove apartment, don't you? That's usually where he takes his women, as I'm sure you know.'

Christian was stunned. Although he'd guessed she'd known that Tony had been unfaithful to her, the knowledge that she was aware of the Coconut Grove apartment struck him like a blow. Had Tony told her? Surely he could not have been that insensitive. He'd been a selfish man all his life but not a cruel one.

Deciding there was no point in lying to her when she'd find out the truth soon enough, he nodded. 'How did you guess?'

Olivia drew a deep breath. 'I couldn't think of any other reason why you might have felt the need to intercede for him,' she said simply. 'As Tony's—deputy, you probably wanted to ensure I wouldn't cause a scene that might embarrass the shareholders.'

Christian caught his breath. 'Is that all you think I care about?' he protested. 'I loved Tony, Olivia. He—he was like a second father to me.'

'I know.' She lifted her shoulders a little wearily. 'Well, don't worry. I won't do anything to cause anyone any distress.'

'Believe it or not, I did not come here because of the company,' Christian exclaimed harshly. 'I offered to give you the news to save you some grief. But I should have realised you'd suspect my motives. That you're too—frigid—to show any normal feelings!'

He regretted the words as soon as they'd left his mouth. Her face, which had been pale before he'd spoken, lost what little colour it had. Her nails dug into her neck, leaving little half-moon scars that were clearly visible. He'd hurt her feelings, no doubt of it. Dammit, after what Tony had put her through, he didn't have the right to criticise her. Despite her unnatural calm, he sensed she was as shocked at the news as he was.

'I think you'd better go,' she said unevenly, gesturing towards the door behind her. 'Joseph will show you out.'

But, if she'd expected the old butler to come to her rescue, she was disappointed. Either the old man had gone back to bed or—more likely—he'd heard enough of what they were saying to realise he should make himself scarce. They were alone—more alone than they'd ever been in all the years he'd known her. So why was he hesitating? He'd done what he came to do.

'Olivia...' Despite himself, Christian took an involuntary step towards her. 'I'm sorry,' he said inadequately, and they both knew he wasn't talking about Tony now.

'It doesn't matter,' she said in return, but there was no conviction in her tone. She put out a hand and he wondered if she expected him to shake it. 'Um—thank you for coming,' she added politely. 'Will you break the news to Luis or shall I?'

'Olivia, for pity's sake!' Christian stared at her. He knew he couldn't leave her like this, but he wasn't foolish enough to think she'd appreciate his concern. 'Let me get you something to drink. There's a wet bar in here, if I remember correctly. You could do with a shot of something to put some colour in your cheeks.'

'I don't need anything.' She spoke firmly, and he heard the unspoken 'from you' although she didn't say those exact words. 'If you want a drink, help yourself. But if you don't mind, I'd like to go back to my room.'

'Not yet.' For reasons he couldn't explain, even to himself, Christian took another step towards her. He could smell her perfume now, a subtle, womanly fragrance that somehow went straight to his head. Or more accurately to his groin, he admitted, conscious of his growing awareness of her frailty. He wanted to comfort her, but that would definitely be a mistake.

Trying to be gentle, he said, 'Olivia, wouldn't you like to talk? I know this must have been a terrible shock to you.'

Olivia held up her head. 'I don't think talking is going to change anything, do you?' she asked, but, although her voice was cool, he could hear the tremor she was trying so hard to disguise. 'You've done your duty, Christian, and I'm grateful. You've warned me what to expect. There's nothing more to say.'

'Olivia!' He was frustrated by his own incompetence. 'I can't leave you like this. I spoke—recklessly. Without thinking. My only excuse is that Tony's death has hit me, too. I need to know that you forgive me.'

'There's nothing to forgive,' she said wearily. 'It's what you were thinking; what you've always thought of me. I know that.'

'But it's not the truth,' Christian exclaimed harshly, aware that he was moving into dangerous waters but unable to stop himself. 'I don't know anything about you, do I? I'm just an ignorant *zoquete* with a big mouth!'

'An oaf?' Olivia recognised the word from things Tony had said. 'I don't think so.' She took a deep breath. 'We both know that Tony wouldn't have had such a high opinion of you if that was so.' She paused. 'Don't beat yourself up over it. This is a difficult time for both of us.'

Christian wasn't reassured. 'Look,' he said, 'whatever you think of me, I don't like this. We both know you're not going to be able to sleep—'

'Because I'm alone?' Her eyes flashed briefly, and he was startled by the sudden candour in her gaze. 'I'm used to sleeping alone, Christian. It's what I do. Tony and I haven't had a real marriage for—well, for a very long time.'

He'd known that, of course. Who better? Tony had trusted him with all his secrets, business and personal. But it was only now that he felt ashamed of being a party to the deception.

He was struck anew by her vulnerability. She

seemed so alone suddenly; so brittle, so fragile—so
unexpectedly desirable that he was stunned by the
sharpness of his need. He wanted her, he realised with
shocked comprehension. He wanted his cousin's
widow. And how despicable was that?

He knew he should get out of there before he did
something totally reprehensible. And with that belief
came the knowledge that his body was hard and
ready. The wonder was that she hadn't noticed his
arousal. But then, she was too much of a lady for
that.

And, as if to strengthen that belief, she closed the
gap between them and touched his hand. 'I'll be fine,'
she said, thankfully misreading his reaction. 'Drive
carefully on your way back. We—we all need you
now.'

Christian stared at her and, before he could prevent
it, his hand covered hers. Her fingers felt so cool, so
soft, and, stifling any misgivings, he brought her hand
to his lips.

He heard her sudden intake of breath as his tongue
skimmed her knuckles, the involuntary jerk she made
as she tried to pull away. But he didn't let go. The
nearness of her lissom body was overwhelming his
good sense and her quickening breath was surely
proof that she wasn't indifferent to him, either.

He didn't stop to think that it might be anger that
was driving her. Need, raw and urgent, was urging
him to take the chance that was being offered to him.
Acting on impulse, he slipped an arm about her waist
and drew her into his embrace.

She was panting now, the rapid tattoo of her heart
visible in the pulse that fluttered below her ear. The
urge to slide his fingers into the neckline of her robe

and feel that racing beat against his palm was almost irresistible, but he restrained himself. Slow down, he told himself, aware that his heart was racing, too. Did he want her to think he was a savage?

'I—think you should go,' she said, her breath moistening his jawline, and for a moment the chance to rescue the situation returned.

'Is that what you want?' he asked, his voice so thick it was barely recognisable to his own ears, and he heard her give a sigh.

'It's what we both want,' she said softly, but he knew it wasn't true.

In any case, it was too late. *Madre de Dios*, it had been too late when he'd touched her. It had probably been too late when he'd first seen her standing in the doorway, looking at him. She'd seemed so incredibly young, so unexpectedly beautiful. And also so defenceless she'd touched his heart.

The tremulous breath that left her lips was both a sign of her confusion and a sensual invitation. His eyes dropped to her breasts, the taut nipples bunched beneath her robe, and his stomach tightened. Dammit, she was as aware of the intimacy of the situation as he was. But had she any idea what a flimsy grip on his control he had?

Her lips parted. 'Christian...' she said, and the appeal in her voice almost persuaded him. 'Let me go.'

But he couldn't do it. His hand against the slippery robe could feel the contradictory heat of her body, the sinuous curve of her spine and the generous swell of her buttocks. The warmth of her arousal rose to his nostrils, mingling with the perfume of her hair, the scent of her skin. And although he knew he was taking advantage of her at a time when she was at her most vulnerable, he couldn't help himself.

His arm tightened automatically bringing her even closer, and her softness soothed his aching erection. *Dios*, it was good to feel her breasts against his chest, her stomach tight against his groin. Unable to prevent himself, he rotated his hips against her and her legs parted in involuntary response to his need.

And, despite the belief that he was damning his soul to perdition, Christian tilted her chin and silenced any further resistance with his mouth.

He felt his senses spiral out of control. Her mouth was just as luscious as he had anticipated. But unexpectedly hot as well. Her lips parted beneath his, inviting his invasion. And, although he could still feel the almost panicked rise and fall of her chest against his shirtfront, the hands that had previously been flexed against his midriff slid away to clutch the sides of his belt, as if for support.

He angled his mouth over hers, his hand cupping her nape, holding her still beneath his hungry assault. His tongue probed every inch of the moist cavern that she offered to him and what had begun as a sensual persuasion became a hungry duel of wills.

The warmth and the scent of her enveloped him and he wondered if she was aware of how very desirable she was. Despite the comparative coolness of the room, beneath her robe he could see that her skin was sheened with sweat. And that excited him. He was already anticipating how her flesh would feel beneath his hands.

His urgency amazed him, his lack of control where she was concerned seemed totally insane. Yet nothing could deny his attraction to her and, fighting his own instincts, he lifted his head.

And found her gazing up at him.

She was staring at him, not with revulsion, as he'd half anticipated, but with a curious mix of wonder and disbelief in her eyes. Those cool grey eyes that had always regarded him with so much hostility were wide now and quizzical, and miraculously free of contempt.

'Why are you doing this?' she asked, her voice low and husky with emotion. 'You don't even like me.'

Didn't he?

Christian wondered if that had ever been true. The way he was feeling now, he couldn't imagine how she could ever have thought such a thing. With the blood pumping hotly through his veins, the question wasn't so much whether he liked her as how he was going to hang on to his reason. In the face of such a strong compulsion, he felt dazed and raw with the need.

As if she understood his dilemma, she added softly, 'I always thought you didn't. I got the feeling you thought I'd only married Tony for his money.'

Tony!

Christian's swimming senses struggled for sanity. *Dios*, what was he doing? He must be crazy. This was Tony's wife; Tony's *widow*! He had just brought her the news that her husband was dead and now he was behaving as if that made her fair game for his carnal appetites. It was unforgivable; he was unforgivable. He had to get out of there before he did something they would both regret.

And yet, when he attempted to put some space between them, a look of confusion crossed her face and her next words gave his tentative withdrawal a totally different motivation. 'It's true, isn't it?' she said, an edge of accusation entering her voice. 'It's what everyone thought. But it wasn't true.'

'I—' For the first time in his life, Christian felt an uncontrollable surge of compassion overwhelming his good sense. 'You're wrong, *querida*,' he told her fiercely. 'You're a beautiful woman. Any man would be proud to have you as his wife.'

'But not Tony?'

'Tony was a fool,' said Christian recklessly, aware of the danger but unable to do anything about it. The intensity of his feelings amazed him. 'And you must know, I was warned to keep my distance from you.'

'Were you?' A little of the pain left her eyes. 'But I think it wasn't so hard for you to keep that promise. I am—how would you say it?—the older woman, yes?'

'You shouldn't equate age with desirability,' he retorted thickly, the hand that had cradled her nape trailing a feather-light caress down her cheek. He felt the sensuous brush of her hair against his skin and his tone harshened with frustration. 'Sex has no barriers.'

'Sex?' She repeated the words almost experimentally and, despite his determination to end this unholy attraction, her soft voice caused the blood to pool hotly in his loins. 'Did you want to have sex with me?' she whispered, the idea obviously new to her. 'Is that what this is all about?'

Dios! What did he say now? Christian gazed down at her with troubled eyes and recognised the uncertainty in her face. And knew he couldn't be less than honest.

'*Dios*, Olivia,' he said, his fingers smoothing the

tender curve of her cheek. 'Of course I want to make love with you. But I don't think this is either the time or the place to be telling you so.'

'Why not? Oh—' Her lips twisted with sudden understanding. 'You mean because of Tony.' A certain bitterness entered her voice. 'Oh, yes, by all means, make Tony your excuse.'

'It's not an excuse,' said Christian, smothering a groan. This was a new experience for him. He had never wanted a woman he couldn't have, but he was no saint and Olivia was so very tempting. '*Querida*, you are upset—distraught. In the morning—'

'In the morning—what?' Although he was sure she didn't realise how provocative the gesture was, she ran her hands over her breasts and down over the voluptuous swell of her hips. 'In the morning I will have to face the press, won't I? I will have to suffer their phony sympathy when I know damn well that what they'll really be doing is rubbing their hands at the prospect of all the newspapers they're going to sell on Tony's back. And when they find out who was with him when he died—' Her lips trembled. 'Well, I'm sure they won't be disappointed at all.' She shrugged. 'Unless Malcolm Sutcliffe gets to their editors first.'

'*Dios*, Olivia…'

His use of her name was both an entreaty and a protest but she wasn't listening to him. With pathetic dignity she stepped away from him, spreading her hands palms down in a silent gesture of defeat. 'I think you'd better go,' she said stiffly. 'It wouldn't do your image any good if you were found here with me.'

Christian swore then, going after her, catching her

arm before she could leave the room. 'Do you honestly think I care about *my* image?' he demanded roughly, and the emotion in his voice seemed to penetrate the wall she was attempting to build between them. '*Dios*, Olivia, what kind of man do you think I am?'

Uncertainty hung in the air between them. 'What kind of man are you?' she asked at last, tremulously, and with a moan of submission Christian pulled her into his arms.

'I am a man who wants you,' he said, abandoning his self-respect along with his reason. '*Te deseo*. I want to be with you.'

CHAPTER SEVEN

OLIVIA spent part of the afternoon sitting at the table in the dining room, trying to make some headway with her writing.

Before Luis's accident, she'd been optimistic about her prospects. She'd mapped out the plots of a series of stories based around the character of a young panda, who had been born in a London zoo, and who had escaped to make his way back to his mother's relatives in China.

It was his—Dimdum's—adventures that she had invented to keep Luis entertained when he was a little boy and, although she'd never actually completed any written work, she had made notes and illustrations over the years, which she'd intended to use now.

Since the accident, however, she'd viewed her efforts with less enthusiasm. Christian's sarcasm about her lack of industry while Tony was alive had struck a chord and she wondered if she wasn't just being a little naïve in thinking she had a talent that could help support her and her unborn child. Would-be authors far exceeded their published counterparts and she didn't kid herself she was any Enid Blyton or Michael Bond.

Nevertheless, she was determined to try and she was soon involved in Dimdum's efforts to persuade a taxi driver to take him to London docks. She was so absorbed, in fact, that she didn't hear the door open behind her, and it wasn't until a shadow fell across the table that she realised someone else was in the room with her.

She lifted her head and immediately felt the hot colour flood into her cheeks. Christian was standing beside her, his eyes on the thumbnail sketch she had drawn to accompany this particular scene. With an exclamation of annoyance, she dragged a clean sheet of paper over her work, successfully hiding it from his view.

Then, unable to keep the resentment out of her voice, she said, 'What do you want?'

Christian's lean dark face took on a wry expression. 'Is that any way to greet a guest?' he protested in pained tones. 'I was just about to compliment you on your artistry. Where did you learn to draw like that?'

Olivia shuffled her papers together with jerky movements. 'I don't think that's any concern of yours,' she replied curtly. 'You made your opinion of my intentions very clear the last time we spoke of it. Now, what is it? Is Luis awake?'

Her stepson usually rested after lunch. His sessions with the physiotherapist invariably tired him and, as he didn't always sleep too well at night, this arrangement suited everyone.

But Christian was not to be diverted. 'Do I take it you've begun writing at last?' he persisted. 'Way to go.'

'Thank you, but I don't need your approval,' retorted Olivia, despising the way his words had cheered her. 'Have you come to tell me you're leaving?'

'No.' Christian turned and propped his hips against the table beside her. Then, a strange expression crossing his face, he said softly, 'Why are you so anxious to get rid of me? Are you afraid I'll tell Luis about us?'

Olivia's jaw dropped. 'There is no ''us'',' she told him, pushing back her chair and getting to her feet. 'And if you're threatening me—'

'I'm not threatening you.' Christian's voice had hardened and he straightened now. 'Olivia, I would never do such a thing.' He paused. 'Surely you know me better than that?'

'But I don't know you, do I?' Olivia countered, even as her pulse quickened at the unwary brush of his arm as she gathered her papers from the table. She took a steadying breath. 'Sorry.'

'*Madre de Dios!*' Her over-politeness seemed to infuriate him. 'We have to work together, Olivia, and you're not helping anything by behaving as if I'm your enemy.'

'Well, you're not my friend,' she declared, holding her manuscript like a shield between them. 'Now, if you don't mind, I'll go and see—'

'I could help you.'

His words were so unexpected that for a moment she could only stare at him. Dear Lord, did he know about the baby? Had he found out? If not, what the hell was he talking about?

She swallowed though her throat was parched. 'I— I beg your pardon?'

'I said, I could help you,' repeated Christian equably. 'I'd like to help you.'

'Help me?' Olivia tried to remain calm. 'How— how could you help me?'

'I have friends in the publishing industry,' he said, nodding towards the manuscript in her arms. 'I could arrange—'

'No!'

Olivia didn't even give herself time to think before refusing his offer. She was trembling now, as much with relief as anything, but she needed to get away from him before her legs gave out on her. Dear God, she could imagine his reaction if she collapsed at his feet. That would really get his attention. But God, for a few moments there, she had been totally convinced he had guessed her secret.

'Olivia!'

'Please…' She couldn't prevent the tremor in her voice but her words were unequivocal. 'I don't want your help. I don't need your help.' And then, although it almost stuck in her throat, 'Thank you.'

He swore then, and if she'd thought her perfunctory gratitude would placate him, she was wrong. 'What is it with you?' he demanded, his face bleak. 'Is it so hard for you to take anything from me? *Por Dios*, I'm not suggesting we climb into bed together again. I'm simply offering you the chance to have your work read by a professional editor instead of it languishing for months in some assistant's slush pile.' He shook his head. 'But, hey, what do I know? You may have a slew of eager editors waiting with bated breath for the first Olivia Mora manuscript!'

Olivia looked down at the papers in her hands. 'There's no need to be sarcastic.'

'Isn't there?' He sounded cynical now. 'No, well, perhaps not. But you don't make this any easier, Olivia. Dammit, what's wrong with me? Why do you hate me so much?'

Olivia almost groaned. 'I—don't hate you.'

'Don't you?'

He was far too close and, despite the fact that she

sensed nothing good would come of trying to appease him, she couldn't move away without inviting further ridicule.

'Look,' she said carefully, 'I don't—that is, I neither like nor dislike you. As I said before, we don't know each other that well. But I just think—after what happened—it's better if we keep our distance.'

'Why?'

'Why?' She blinked at him.

'Yes, why?' he asked her again. 'What do we have to lose by spending time together?'

Olivia's tongue made a weak foray over her lips. 'I—because—because it's very difficult for us to behave—naturally with one another.'

Christian lifted his shoulders in a careless gesture. 'It's not difficult for me.'

Obviously not.

Olivia swallowed again and tried another tack. 'Whatever you say, I know you don't really like me,' she said firmly, and he gave a short laugh.

'And what have I ever done to make you think that?'

'Oh—' She moved her head helplessly from side to side. 'This is ridiculous.'

'I agree.'

'No. I mean this conversation,' she muttered, wishing she could think of some clever retort to wipe the smug expression off his face. 'What do you want from me?'

'Ah, that's a better question.'

She sighed in the face of the faint smile that tilted his lips. 'You know what I mean.'

'Do I?' He frowned then. 'Why do I have to want anything? I've offered to help you with your writing, but you don't want that. I've provided you with transport, whether you choose to take advantage of it or not. I've done what I can to show you that my visit here is wholly innocent of any hidden motive, but for some reason you refuse to accept that I might have wanted to see Luis for myself. I have to ask myself why.'

Olivia shook her head. This was getting her nowhere fast. Everything she said, every move she made, was geared towards making him feel so uncomfortable here that he'd be glad to leave, but it wasn't working. On the contrary, it was making him question her motives, and that was something she didn't want to do.

She wondered how she'd have felt if she weren't expecting his child; if the night they'd spent together had ended for her, as it had for him, when he'd got in his car and driven away. Would she have felt such animosity towards him then or might she have been flattered by his sudden appearance, by his apparent desire to make amends?

It was incredibly easy to see what had drawn her to him. With every move he made, he exuded an air of latent sexuality, which was as natural to him as it was potent to her. She couldn't help but be aware of him, of what they had shared, and as the muscles in her stomach clenched convulsively she conceded that her resentment of him was couched in the knowledge of her own unholy attraction to him.

But, as if he had at last grown tired of baiting her, Christian ended the standoff. 'All right,' he said, spreading his hands, and against her will her eyes were ensnared by the curl of dark hair visible above the neckline of his tank-top. 'I give in. I'll stay out of your way in future. But I can't leave tonight. It's too late. I'll tell Luis I'm catching tomorrow morning's ferry.'

Olivia nodded. 'If that's what you want.'

Christian muttered an oath then. 'It's not what I want,' he snapped harshly. 'It's what you want. I had hoped we might be able to mend some fences here, but that's not your style. You've got it into your head that I made love to you for some selfish motive of my own, and whatever I say you're going to twist my words.'

Despite herself, a shiver feathered down Olivia's spine at the memory. But she had to set the record straight.

'We didn't—make love,' she declared in a low voice. 'We had sex, that was all. I accept that we were both in a state of shock and that neither of us really considered what we were doing. But it's—changed things, that's all. Changed things between us,' she added hastily. 'I thought you'd understand.'

Christian stared at her with impatient eyes. 'That's your opinion, is it?'

She hesitated only a moment. 'Yes.'

'Well, you're wrong,' he told her roughly. 'Oh, I understand what you're trying to say, what you're trying to do, but it wasn't like that between us. Okay, maybe it was inspired by a need to assert our own survival in the face of grim mortality, but it wasn't just sex. And if that's what this is all about, then you got it wrong.'

Olivia caught her breath. 'Does it matter?' she exclaimed, anxious to put an end to this. It was much easier for her to go on believing that Christian was a bastard than to admit that he might be feeling any remorse over what had happened. It made him far too sympathetic, far too human. 'Look—it happened. And we both regret it. Isn't it better if we keep away from one another from now on?'

Christian gave her an old-fashioned look. 'Why? In case we get the need to jump one another again?'

'No!' She was defensive. 'But we don't want Luis to get the wrong idea.'

'Which would be?'

She made a dismissive gesture. 'Well, that we're having an affair, of course.'

'Oh, right.' Christian's lips twisted. 'And you're not afraid he's going to get suspicious when I tell him you want me to leave?'

'You don't have to tell him I've asked you to leave,' protested Olivia irritably. And then, 'I—oh, please yourself what you do,' she muttered, pushing him aside and making for the door. 'Excuse me. I've got things to do.'

It was galling to find that Luis was still resting and, feeling too stressed to go out in the hot afternoon sun, Olivia was forced to retire to her room. But, once there, with her manuscript safely locked in the drawer of her bureau, she couldn't sit still. Despite herself, Christian's interpretation of what had happened the night Tony died had stirred unwilling memories inside her, and until she dealt with them she wasn't going to be able to relax.

The trouble was, his conception of how it had been between them was so different from the picture she had built up over the weeks and months since it had happened. It had been so much simpler to paint him as the villain, to pretend that she'd played no active role in her own downfall.

But it wasn't true. He hadn't taken advantage of her any more than she had taken advantage of him. He was right. She had been ripe for seduction, a seduction she had wanted just as much as he had...

Yet it hadn't started out that way.

She was lying awake, watching the play of light from the moon outside etching patterns on the ceiling above her bed, when Joseph knocked at her door.

The old butler was her friend and Olivia knew he wouldn't have disturbed her unless he had something important to tell her. When he explained that Mr Rodrigues was downstairs, she felt the first glimmerings of foreboding. And apprehension, too. What could Christian Rodrigues want with her?

His image, lean, dark, and uncomfortably intense, flashed into her mind. Christian Rodrigues was nothing if not disturbing, his black eyes and sinuous body a challenge to every woman he met. Olivia had never liked him, aware that he probably felt the same about her. But that hadn't stopped her from noticing him, or from admitting, albeit scornfully, that the man was as sexy as sin.

And as dangerous, she acknowledged, wondering what he was doing here in the middle of the night. If he expected to find Tony here, he was mistaken. Tony only stayed at the Bal Harbour house if they had hosted a party or a reception. Even then, he had his own room. And Joseph was perfectly aware of that.

As Christian was, too, she conceded flatly, pulling her silk wrapper over her nightgown. Which meant this probably wasn't something Tony would want to know about. Oh, God, what had Luis done now?

She thought about getting dressed and then dismissed the notion. Christian wouldn't care what she looked like and it wasn't as if he hadn't seen a woman in a dressing gown before. If she went down stark naked, she doubted if he'd notice her. Which was the way she wanted it, she told herself. She was too old to worry about what he thought of her now.

He was waiting for her in the living room. Although it was a large room, it was still considerably smaller than the formal reception rooms that adjoined it. He was standing staring out of the windows and for a moment she allowed herself to look at him unseen.

He seemed much bigger than she remembered, but that was probably because she hadn't stopped to put on shoes or slippers. His back, broad and uncompromising, was clad less formally than usual. He wasn't wearing a jacket, for one thing, and a narrow arrow of sweat darkened his shirt.

Her pulse quickened in spite of herself. She wondered how she'd have felt if he'd come here to see her personally. But despite the fact that Tony had broken his marriage vows many times, he expected her to be constant. He'd warned her that she'd never see Luis again if she was unfaithful to him.

Which she had no desire to be, she assured herself, despite the little frisson of awareness she felt when Christian turned towards her. She didn't know what was the matter with her. It must be the fact that it was the middle of the night and for once Christian looked less than sure of himself. His dark hair was unruly, as if he'd been running his hands through it, and he obviously hadn't shaved since that morning. There was the shadow of night-dark stubble along his jaw.

She felt a tremor run through her. Something was wrong. She knew it. Her heart skipped a beat. Dear God, Luis had only left for the west coast a few weeks ago. Surely nothing bad had happened to him.

And yet...

The news when it came was both better and worse. Luis was all right, but Tony was dead. He'd had a heart attack, Christian said, while he was with his latest mistress. He'd probably died humping her, thought Olivia bitterly. Wasn't that what always happened to men who refused to act their age?

Christian, meanwhile, was far too understanding. Which was why she dismissed his concern for her as a ploy to save the company's image. In the circumstances, it would be far too easy to lean on him, to misinterpret his kindness as something more than sympathy. Too easy to let him become the rock she'd never had.

But instead of arousing his contempt, she sparked his temper. He ended up accusing her of being frigid, which was probably the way he thought of her anyway. Whatever, she wanted him to go before she said or did something stupid. She felt surprisingly vulnerable and she wished Joseph would come back and she could ask him to show Christian out.

But Joseph had disappeared, and she wondered if the old butler thought Christian's arrival had been expected. Perhaps he thought she was going to give Tony a taste of his own medicine. As if, she thought, rather wistfully, knowing she should feel betrayed. But it was much too late for that.

She didn't honestly know how she did feel: sorry, of course, definitely. But the Tony she'd married was not the Tony she'd believed him to be. It was like hearing of the death of a close acquaintance, sad, but not devastating. She'd loved him once, but no longer. He'd killed her love years ago.

Even so, she was surprised to hear herself confiding in Christian. She never would have thought she'd confess the circumstances of her marriage to him. She guessed he'd known it anyway. As he was Tony's second-in-command, it would have been impossible for him not to have realised what was going on.

Yet, when she touched Christian's hand, she had no conception of what she was unleashing. She'd wanted to comfort him, to show him she'd forgiven him, but the situation between them was much too intense for that. Before she knew what was happening she was in his arms and, although she made a perfunctory protest, the feel of his hard body against hers was far too disturbing to dismiss.

The pull of her need was frightening. For so long she'd endured her celibacy in silence, ignoring the natural demands of her body, believing herself free of the sexual urges that governed other people's lives. She knew Tony's women believed she was frigid and, in truth, she'd begun to believe they might be right. But when Christian's hand curved over her bottom, drawing her close to his unmistakable erection, her inner alarm was silenced by the rush of her desire.

She so much wanted him to touch her, not just where he was touching now but in other places that were hot and wet and pulsing with anticipation. He smelled so good—soap and sweat and body heat. And the musky scent of his arousal, that was male and vital, and driving her insane.

She suspected he was as shocked by her response as she was. She didn't know what he'd expected when he'd fastened his mouth to hers, but it wasn't the wild surrender he received. For a moment, she gave in to her needs; indulged her desires. Then common sense and decency caused him to draw back and she realised he was embarrassed by her lack of restraint.

When he made the excuse about Tony, she was mortified, as much by his loyalty as her behaviour. What must he think of her, she wondered, lusting after her husband's deputy? Dear God, she didn't know what was happening to her. But somehow she had to salvage this before something completely disastrous occurred.

With a belated attempt at dignity, she asked him to go. As he said, she was in a state of shock. She couldn't be blamed for her actions. She'd needed sympathy and he'd given it. Anything else was pure fantasy. His words, his reassurances, his actions, had all been designed to restore her self-respect.

'I don't think it would do your image any good to be found here with me,' she said stiffly, turning away. 'I'll find Joseph...'

Christian swore then, catching her arm before she could leave the room. 'Do you honestly think I care about *my* image?' he demanded, and the emotion in his voice breached the wall she'd built around herself. 'What kind of a man do you think I am?'

The uncertainty in the air was vibrant. 'What kind of man are you?' she whispered, and with a groan of anguish Christian pulled her into his arms.

'I am a man who wants you,' he said, and her legs went weak beneath her. '*Te deseo*. I want to be with you.'

It couldn't be happening; it *shouldn't* be happening. But it was. Christian's mouth on hers was hot and urgent and unbelievably sensual. She found herself opening to him, her tongue coming to meet his in a dance as old as time. Submission or seduction, it didn't matter. With her hands spread against his back, she was careless of the distinction. She just wanted him to go on loving her, warming her aching heart.

He drew back once, his hand cupping her jaw, his thumb brushing roughly over her lower lip that was swollen from his kisses. His eyes searched hers, caressed hers, seemed to find what he was looking for in their silvery depths. Then, in a thick voice, he said, 'Can we go upstairs, *querida*? Or don't you think Donelli will come back?'

Almost in a dream, it seemed, Olivia took his hand and led him up the stairs. Her room—the room that had once been the master bedroom and was now so much less than that—was as she'd left it. Cream satin-covered pillows, edged with lace, were tumbled on cream satin sheets. The coverlet lay at the foot of the bed, where the maid had turned it, its neat green and cream folds an indication of how little she used the space.

The room was quite warm, but Olivia shivered. Apart from Tony, she had never allowed any man into her bed. She didn't even know how good at this she was. If Tony was any judge, she was probably as hopeless at sex as she was at keeping her husband.

But her husband was dead...

The chilling thought caused another wave of goose-bumps to prickle her skin. But, as though Christian knew what she was thinking, he cupped her face between his fingers. Then, rubbing his lips against hers, he rekindled the startling fire she'd felt before coming upstairs.

'Are you cold?' he asked softly, and suddenly she felt warm and excited. His dark eyes were caressing her, convincing her he found her as attractive as he'd said. It might not be true, but for the moment she was too aroused to care if he was lying to her. He wanted her. That much was obvious. She could feel his throbbing heat against her hip.

'Are you?' she countered daringly, looking up at him, and with an exclamation in his own language he allowed his hands to slide softly down her back. They slid beneath the neckline of her robe, warm against her shoulders. Her skin felt slick with perspiration, but he didn't seem to care.

'What do you think?' he asked at last, and she wondered if she dared pull his shirt out of the waistband of his trousers. She wanted to feel his skin, flesh against flesh. But it was so long since she'd shared this intimacy, and Christian was a totally unknown entity.

'I think you're very warm,' she said shyly, and his smile was suddenly devastating.

'I think I am, too,' he said, saving her the effort by freeing his own shirt from his trousers. He tore the buttons open, not caring that one popped off and went skittering across the floor. 'Yeah,' he said at last, pulling her against him, 'that's better.' His mouth caressed her earlobes, his breath quickening unevenly. 'But it's not as good as it gets.'

She didn't understand him, but when the sides of her robe gaped suddenly she realised he'd released the belt that held it at her waist. Beneath, the pale green satin nightgown left nothing to his imagination. The dark circles around her breasts were clearly visible, the smoky shadow between her legs no longer any mystery to him.

Her embarrassment was instant, but his next words disarmed her completely. 'You are so beautiful,' he said, holding the sides of the robe apart and feasting his eyes on her. '*Dios, querida,* I think you want me. Why did I never realise that before?'

Because it wasn't true, she thought wildly, suddenly ashamed of the emotions she was feeling. And she wasn't beautiful. Tony had convinced her of that. He had ensured she wore the most expensive clothes, that she looked elegant when he wanted her to. But he had never said she was beautiful. How could she believe it now?

Yet, when Christian's eyes lingered on her, she felt unexpectedly sexy. The satin nightgown clung in all the right places and she was glad she wasn't wearing the vest and boxers she sometimes wore to bed. She felt young—not as young as Christian perhaps, but not middle-aged, either—and attractive. And so amazingly alive she felt as if she were floating on air.

When he slipped the robe off her shoulders, so that it pooled about their feet, she quivered. And when his hands gripped her waist and brought her against him, all she was aware of was the look of pure possession in his eyes. She felt a sharp and totally unfamiliar desire to be naked with him, and she didn't mind at all when her nightgown followed her robe onto the floor.

It was years since she'd stood naked before any man. The brief honeymoon of a marriage she and Tony had shared had ended all too soon and his indifference to anyone's feelings but his own had destroyed their relationship. Was that when she'd conceived the notion that she was less of a woman because of it? Had she allowed Tony's unfaithfulness to colour the image she had of herself?

It was a thought, but right now she didn't much care about her image. With Christian's eyes upon her, she felt beautiful even if she wasn't. He was looking at her intently, the unmistakable gleam of hunger in his gaze. He wanted her. Suddenly she believed it. He desired her and her legs went weak at the thought.

As if sensing her surrender, Christian backed her gently towards the bed. But he was still wearing far too many clothes. Giving in to the unfamiliar stranger who had taken over her body, she reached determinedly for his belt.

Before she could do more than tug on his buckle, however, the backs of her legs hit the side of the bed and she subsided rather ungracefully onto the sheets. But it didn't matter anyway because Christian came down beside her, kicking off his shoes as he joined her on the bed.

'Aren't you going to take off your clothes?' she protested, her breathing quickening as he bestowed a sensuous kiss on the slope of her breast.

'You'd better believe it,' he said, his hands cupping her ribcage with sensual possession. His thumbs rubbed the undersides of her breasts until she wriggled with frustration. 'Take it easy,' he added softly. 'We have all night.'

Moving with sinuous grace, he straddled her, and although he was still wearing his trousers there was no mistaking the fact that he was sexually aroused. Unable to help herself she ran her fingers over the swell of his erection, and he groaned in protest before spreading her hands above her head.

'All in good time,' he said, his voice revealing the control he was having to exert upon himself. He released one hand and scraped his thumb over one sensitive peak. Her breast hardened instantly, and she twisted beneath him. 'You like that, *querida*?' he whispered. 'Tell me. I want to know exactly how you feel.'

'I feel—wanton,' she said, her breath catching helplessly. 'And I want you to touch me—just as much as I want to touch you.' She held his eyes as with her freed hand she released the zip on his pants. Then, despite his instinctive protest, she slipped her hand inside.

Silk boxers clung to her fingers but the turgid heat of his shaft was eager to escape. '*Por favor*, Olivia,' he choked as she slipped her hand around him. 'I want this to be good for you and if you continue to do that—' He drew an unsteady breath. '*Dios*, I am only human, *entiende*?'

'I know.'

Her voice was soft and with an exclamation he unbuckled his belt and quickly pushed off his trousers. The black boxers quickly followed them, joining the rest of their clothes on the floor.

Now, with no barriers between them, he kissed her, his lips lingering on hers, his tongue pushing greedily into her mouth. With evident satisfaction he explored every corner of that moist cavern before encouraging her to follow his lead.

And she did, only to have him draw her tongue between his teeth and suck on it strongly. The sensual friction caused a constriction in her throat and a liquid rush of heat that spread throughout her body. She felt a pain in the pit of her stomach and an ache between her legs that wouldn't go away.

His chest hair brushed her breasts and, with his throbbing erection against her belly, she wanted him inside her so bad, she didn't know how she could stand any more. She moaned when he drew back, arching up towards him, and saw the raw desire in his face.

He trailed his tongue down between her breasts, depositing wet little kisses as he did so that only intensified her need. He paused to massage a nipple between his thumb and forefinger, and then transferred his attention to the neglected one before taking it into his mouth.

He sucked again, and this time she felt the pull deep inside her womb. Oh, God, did he have any idea what he was doing to her? She was already on the edge of an orgasm, already far beyond the point of no return.

But, as if he had no conception of how fragile her control was, he drew back to continue his tongue's tantalising exploration. His hand slid over her belly, invading the damp curls at the apex of her legs. He found the tender nub of her desire and rubbed his thumb against it. And then slid a finger inside her and she was lost.

As her body shook with her climax, and she moaned at the realisation that he had not shared her pleasure, Christian bent to kiss her lips again, his satisfaction clear.

'Was it good?' he asked huskily, and she nodded in helpless assent.

'But you didn't—'

'That was for you,' he said softly. Then, before she

could voice another protest, he slid over her and into her and she caught her breath as he added huskily, 'This is for us both.'

His thick shaft filled her completely, her muscles stretching to accommodate his size. 'Tight,' he said with satisfaction. 'I knew you would be. I could almost believe you've never been with a man before.'

Olivia trembled. She hadn't known sex could be like this, hadn't known there could be so much pleasure, so much enjoyment to be shared. And what she definitely wasn't prepared for was how she would feel when he began to move inside her, stroking nerves she hadn't known she possessed.

Unbelievably she felt her body beginning to respond again. She gazed up into his lean, arresting face, seeing his heavy-lidded eyes darken with concentration, felt the damp strands of his hair that were plastered to his nape cling to her fingers when she clutched his neck.

Her climax came as he slid his hands down between them, drawing her legs even wider apart, penetrating to the very core of her being. And was overtaken by his own release, when he collapsed, shuddering, in her arms...

CHAPTER EIGHT

OLIVIA sank down onto the window seat now, staring blindly out at the deepening shadows of late afternoon. It was the first time she had allowed herself to recall the events of that night in any detail and it disturbed her to acknowledge at last that Christian had been no more to blame for what had happened than she had.

Perhaps less so, she conceded painfully, remembering how achingly needy she had been. It was easy to make the excuse that she had been more vulnerable, that Christian had been more experienced. But in truth she had initiated what had happened; she had invited Christian into her bed.

She pressed a hand to her stomach to still the tremor that rippled over her womb at this admission. Dear God, what was she supposed to do now? Did it mean she had to tell Christian about the baby? Tell a man, who at best regarded her as a necessary encumbrance, that she was expecting his child?

No!

She couldn't do it. Couldn't expose herself like that. He had his own life and she had hers. She didn't want Christian to feel any responsibility for something he could only regard as a mistake.

Nevertheless, she had to stop behaving as if he were her enemy. She could see now that that could only create the kind of friction she was trying to avoid. Besides, she realised now that it was her unwanted attraction to Christian that was causing her the most soul-searching. She wanted to hate him; she wanted to blame him. But she couldn't.

However, until Luis was on his feet again, she had to bite the bullet and behave as if Christian's presence were an unexpected complication and nothing more. Analysing her feelings hadn't solved her problems. It had only clarified them. And she could now see how pathetic she had been in imagining she had things under control.

In this new light of revelation she accepted that she had a lot to thank Christian for. It was he who had flown to California to break the news about Tony to Luis. He who had kept the hordes of reporters at bay until the police had released Tony's body for burial.

Despite Senator Sutcliffe's best efforts, his wife's relationship with Tony Mora had eventually been exposed, but Olivia had refused any interviews that would have involved condemning her husband's behaviour. Instead, she had remained unnaturally aloof, hiding her own feelings behind a wall of silence, earning herself the label of the frozen widow.

She sighed, and, deciding she ought to start as she meant to go on, she went to take a shower before dressing for the evening meal. She chose her favourite silk shorts and a hip-length tunic of pale green chiffon. It was the kind of cool and flimsy outfit she'd have worn if she'd been alone.

Yet as she smoothed an amber eye-shadow onto her lids she wondered if she'd chosen it arbitrarily or deliberately. Her bra was clearly visible through the gauzy fabric, her breasts fuller than they used to be, spilling over the lacy cups. She assured herself it was no more daring than the vest and briefs she'd been wearing that morning when Christian had met her on the beach. But the suspicion remained that she was testing him. And how pathetic was that?

Her hair was still damp after her shower so she secured it at her nape with a leather thong. Then, after slipping heelless sandals onto her feet, she joined Susannah in the kitchen to discuss what they were going to have for supper that evening.

As it happened, Luis was in a foul mood when he joined them. The civilised meal Olivia had planned deteriorated into a series of arguments between her stepson, his nurse, and Christian, and the delicious soft-shelled crabs and grilled red snapper went virtually unremarked.

Luis's excuse, that his hip was itching unbearably and that he was sick of being confined to the villa, didn't earn him much sympathy, but it was only when Christian mentioned that he was thinking of going back to Miami the next day that Luis really lost his cool.

'I thought you told me you were planning on staying a few days,' he accused the older man angrily. 'What's happened? What's Mom been saying to you?' He turned his irate gaze on Olivia. 'For God's sake, Mom, can't you put your own selfish feelings aside for once and think of me?'

'Luis!'

Christian uttered a harsh exclamation that overrode Olivia's automatic reproach. 'Do not speak to your mother like that, *chico*,' he warned, his lean face dark and dangerously intent. 'If it wasn't for Olivia, you would be spending your days with paid nursing staff to care for you. You wouldn't be living in these surroundings, waited on hand and foot. You are an ungrateful pup and I am ashamed of you.'

'Hey, I don't need your approval—' began Luis, apparently prepared to bluff it out, but Christian wasn't finished with him yet.

'Oh, you do,' he contradicted him bleakly. 'Your mother may be your guardian until you are twenty-one. But I am an executor of your father's will, and unless you change your ways and start acting like a responsible adult I may have to revise my opinion of the generous allowance you are presently paid to do f—'

Christian broke off at this point, faint colour entering his cheeks at his imminent lapse of control. But his meaning was clear, and although Luis huffed a bit he knew he was treading on dangerous ground.

'Anyway,' he muttered as Helen Stevens made some excuse about helping Susannah clear the table and took herself off, 'I do appreciate what Mom's done for me. I do. I'm not a complete moron. I know she's been great. But that doesn't alter the fact that I was looking forward to you staying on for a few more days. I thought we might go sailing or something. You've got the Jeep. We could go down to the docks. Maybe hire ourselves a catamaran. God, I need male company, man! I'm living here with three women and it sucks.'

Christian's expression hardly changed. 'I think you should watch your language, *man*,' he said, no trace of sympathy in his tone, and Olivia expelled a nervous sigh.

'In any case, I don't think Helen would sanction your riding around in a Jeep until the doctor says so,' she put in unhappily. 'It has been just a month, Luis.'

'Yeah?' Luis's chin wobbled for a moment. 'I know exactly how long it's been, Mom. Thirty-two days and counting.'

'Luis—'

'You're feeling sorry for yourself, is all,' Christian inserted before Olivia could start defending herself. 'And let's not forget, you have only yourself to blame. According to the highway cops out in California, you were driving well above the accepted speed limit. Well above. You're lucky you didn't kill yourself.'

'Lucky, yeah,' muttered Luis bitterly, but it was obvious all the aggression had drained out of him and Olivia felt herself weakening.

'Look,' she said awkwardly, 'I've got no objections if—if Christian wants to change his mind and stay on for a few more days.' She felt Christian's eyes upon her, but she couldn't meet his gaze. 'Of course, he may have other plans...' Her voice trailed away. 'But if not...'

'You don't have to do this, Olivia.' Christian's words required her to turn and look at him and she saw the wary uncertainty in his face. 'Luis is having a bad day. He'll get over it.'

'Nevertheless...' Olivia spoke quickly before she had time to think what she was doing and have second thoughts. 'If you'd like to stay, you can. I don't mind.'

Christian frowned. 'Olivia—'

'Hey, she says you can stay,' broke in Luis desperately, obviously seeing this second chance slipping away, too. 'Come on, Chris. Do it. I know I've been acting like a klutz and I'm sorry. Give me a break here, can't you? I promise I won't do anything else stupid. Please! Say you'll stay.'

'Well…' Christian looked at Olivia again and this time she couldn't prevent the wave of hot colour that rose up into her throat at his insistent appraisal. 'If you're sure about this?'

She swallowed. 'I am,' she said firmly, getting up from the table and gathering the empty dishes together. 'Excuse me. I need to go and see how the others are getting on.'

Why had she done it?

Christian was still pondering the reasons why Olivia might have changed her mind the next morning. She'd been so eager to be rid of him, so adamant that he should leave. Had she only asked him to stay to pacify her stepson? Or was she beginning to believe he wasn't as black as he'd been painted?

He knew Tony's attitude towards him had done him no favours. The older man had got a kick out of telling everyone they were so alike. It wasn't true. Christian had never been as promiscuous as his cousin. And, although he'd had his share of girl-friends, he'd never slept with a woman he hadn't had some feelings for.

His relationship with Olivia had often been a rocky one. She had always been suspicious of his motives for coming to work for Tony. And, for his part, he'd been obliged to keep his distance from her because of what Tony had said. Which hadn't seemed such a hardship until the night Tony died…

He sighed. What had happened that night? Oh, it was easy to find excuses for his behaviour, even if his conscience wouldn't let it rest. Olivia had been distressed and he'd comforted her. But in the process he'd given himself a problem he couldn't seem to solve.

And that was some admission. Particularly after the way she'd treated him since Tony died. She couldn't have made her contempt for him clearer if she'd tried. She didn't like him and she lost no opportunity to inform him of the fact.

Nevertheless, something happened when they were together, he argued. And he wasn't the only one who was aware of it, either. Even at the hospital, after Luis had had his accident, he'd sensed the panic she'd felt when he'd touched her. Why was she afraid of him? What did she have to hide?

He'd have liked to think it was because she was unwillingly attracted to him. But he was afraid that was pushing the envelope too far. He knew she wasn't experienced with men and she was probably dealing with what had happened the only way she knew how. He was really fooling himself if he believed she had any other reason to keep him at arm's length.

The real problem was, he was attracted to her. He'd always been aware of her, of course, but so long as Tony was alive he'd respected his cousin's desire to keep other men at bay. He wasn't into having affairs with married women, even if she'd been willing. She might not believe it, but Christian had never done anything he was seriously ashamed of before.

And he wasn't really ashamed of what had happened the night Tony died, he acknowledged ruefully. He couldn't have kissed her as he had, couldn't have made love to her so eagerly, without the strong feelings she'd aroused in him that night. The trouble was, those feelings hadn't gone away. They were still bug-

ging him. That was the underlying reason why he'd
made this trip to San Gimeno. He'd wanted to see if
he'd been exaggerating their importance to him.

And, hey, what do you know? he thought bitterly.
He hadn't. They were still alive and kicking him in
the gut. That was why his relationship with Julie had
foundered. Which was really pathetic considering the
way Olivia felt about him.

Yet even she couldn't deny the electricity there was
between them. Dammit, even Luis had noticed they
struck sparks off one another every time they met.
That was one of the reasons why he found her company so exhilarating. He enjoyed being with her. He
was never bored when they were together. He never
found himself looking at his watch or wishing he
were some place else.

But how to persuade her of that presented him with
an almost insoluble problem. Okay, she'd agreed to
let him stay on for a few days, but how significant
was that? He'd have to go back to Miami at the end
of the week whatever happened. He couldn't leave
Mike Delano holding the fort indefinitely. And then
when would he see her again? What possible excuse
could he make for coming back?

He'd half expected her to have had her breakfast
and gone before he entered the sunlit morning room.
But she was still sitting at the table, holding a cup of
coffee and staring blindly out at the view when he
came in. In the moment before she became aware of
his presence, he studied her averted face almost
greedily. And felt the recurring stab of desire he'd
been trying to suppress.

Dios, he chided himself, schooling his features as
she heard his intake of breath and turned to look at

him. What in God's name was happening to him? Where had this sudden hunger come from? When had he stopped regarding her as an older woman? When had she become this disturbing creature who filled his nights with tormented dreams?

'Good morning,' she said, her polite greeting cutting his ego down to size.

He grunted a response, gratefully taking the chair opposite before she could see how she affected him. Then applied himself to the basket of warm rolls she pushed towards his plate.

But that didn't stop him from watching her as she poured a cup of coffee and offered him cream and sugar. 'Just black. Thank you,' he added, almost belatedly. But he didn't like this feeling of inadequacy. It took some getting used to.

Olivia was wearing pink this morning: pale pink tee shirt, with the logo of a friendly dolphin splashed across her breasts; pink shorts, that revealed a delightful length of leg, and a broad pink hair band, that complemented the warm tan that tinted her features and left her silvery-gold hair loose about her shoulders.

She looked so young, he thought incredulously. So wholesome. He'd never seen a woman who looked so good without make-up before. It made him despise the carnal thoughts he'd been having about her. But it didn't stop him from wanting to make her notice him.

'Is the coffee still hot?'

The businesslike tone of her words showed him she was doing her best to be civil with him. It was the kind of thing a good hostess would say. But in spite of the warnings he'd been giving himself, he couldn't help resenting her cool approach.

'Do you care?' he asked, deliberately provoking her. 'We both know you only invited me to stay on to get Luis off your back.'

For a moment, he thought she was going to deny it. Her lips parted in surprise and it took her a moment to formulate her response. But then her expression changed and Christian found himself regretting his crassness. It wasn't her fault he couldn't control his libido.

'That didn't stop you from accepting my offer,' she said at last, evidently deciding against trying to persuade him otherwise. 'I had hoped we might be able to achieve a working relationship, but evidently I was wrong.'

Christian shrugged, still finding it difficult to silence his demons. 'I'm willing to call a truce,' he said. He arched a mocking brow. 'What kind of a "working relationship" did you have in mind?'

It was uncouth and it was suggestive, and he wasn't really surprised when she didn't dignify it with a reply. Instead, she pushed back her chair and got to her feet, and started across the room towards the open windows. It would serve him right if she chucked him out, he thought. He was the world's biggest jerk and he knew it.

'*Dios*, Olivia—' he muttered as she reached the threshold of the veranda. But although she must have heard his protest, she didn't look back. With another exclamation, this time less polite, he thrust back his chair and went after her, pausing only briefly when he saw her braced against the veranda rail.

She had her back to him, and his first reaction was

to think how delicious her rounded bottom looked in the hot pink shorts. But then, squashing that thought, he crossed the slats between them, halting right behind her and trying to steady his breath.

'Olivia,' he said again, this time with real feeling, and she swung round and pressed her hips against the barrier, evidently surprised to find that he was so close. Her lips were pressed together tightly and her eyes were wide and guarded. She looked like a rabbit in the headlights of an oncoming vehicle. Frozen to the spot, yet desperate to get away.

'I'm sorry,' he said, eager to make amends for his behaviour. But his apology only served to bring her back to life. Shaking her head, she would have left him then, probably in pursuit of either the housekeeper or her stepson for protection. But Christian gripped the rail at either side of her, successfully imprisoning her between his hands.

'Don't you believe me?' he asked, and, hearing himself say the words, he was amazed at how desperate he sounded now. '*Querida*,' he continued, 'I didn't mean to be rude. I didn't mean to hurt you. I'm useless and I don't deserve anything else.'

To his surprise, Olivia didn't respond as he'd anticipated. He'd half expected her to dismiss his plea and insist that he let her go at once. Instead, a faint smile touched her lips and he could see that she was amused by his choice of words.

'You're not useless and you know it,' she said lightly, pressing a finger into his chest, possibly in the hope that he'd move away. 'Now, please, I've got work to do. Luis hasn't had his breakfast yet.'

Christian was tempted to say, To hell with Luis, but he wasn't out of the wood yet. And although com-

mon sense demanded that he consider himself fortu-
nate to be let off so easily, he was acutely aware of
her finger digging into his flesh.

'So you forgive me?' he persisted, feeling her
warm breath moistening the skin above his tank-top.
It was another connection; another link between them.
It wasn't something he wanted, but he was still getting aroused.

Olivia withdrew her finger abruptly, as if the heat
he was generating had communicated itself to her,
and this time her smile was a little forced as she said,
'What's to forgive?'

It was an instinctive response, made in the hope
that he'd accept it and let her go. She was shifting
from foot to foot, a sure sign that she was nervous,
and he was amazed at how innocent she seemed even
now.

'How about we put everything that's gone before
behind us and start again?' he suggested softly, only
resisting the urge to trace the curve of her jawline
with his tongue by a supreme effort. 'I'd like us to
be friends.' Hell, he'd like a lot more than that if he
were honest. 'I know we started out badly, but I'd
really like for us to get to know one another properly.'

It should have reassured her, but it didn't seem to.
Despite the fact that he was putting real energy into
gaining her confidence, she still seemed as skittish as
a colt.

'We'll see,' she said at last, wrapping her arms
across her chest and tucking her fingers beneath her
arms. 'But I really can't talk about it now. Like I said
before, I've got things to do.'

Christian's mouth flattened. 'Like what?' he asked,
flexing his hands on the wooden guardrail instead of

giving in to a desire to smooth his fingertips over the soft skin of her arms. 'Getting Luis's breakfast? I thought Helen took care of that.'

'Well, she does.' There was no doubt that Olivia was frustrated now. 'But I always go and see how he's feeling before he gets out of bed.'

Lucky Luis, thought Christian drily, his eyes intent on her anxious face. The heat that had flooded her throat earlier had now worked its way into her face and hectic spots of colour highlighted her cheeks.

'Okay,' he said at last, deciding he'd gain nothing from baiting her, despite the wicked pleasure in the deed. Her lips parted as he stepped back and he was almost tempted to change his mind. Had she no idea how provocative licking her lips was?

Obviously not. Or how revealing her agitation seemed as the saucy dolphin on her tee shirt danced nervously up and down. Her nipples were hard—a possible reaction to her panic? Or an arousal she was trying quite hard to hide?

Christian couldn't be sure. He'd have liked to think she was becoming aware of the energy between them that had found its own release the night Tony died. But for so long she'd ignored him, remained aloof from any man but Luis, that she probably found it hard to relax with him.

She moved away from the rail now, edging sideways past him, clearly hoping he wouldn't try to delay her again. 'I'll—I'll see you later,' she said, and Christian thrust his hands into the pockets of his shorts to disguise his erection.

'You'd better believe it,' he added, and she gave a nod before hurriedly slipping away.

CHAPTER NINE

IT WASN'T easy avoiding Christian.

The villa, which had seemed almost spacious when Olivia was living alone, seemed to shrink in size by the day. Besides, avoiding Christian often meant avoiding Luis, and she couldn't let her stepson think that anything was wrong.

On the whole, Luis had never seemed happier. It was an odd conclusion for her to make, considering he was recovering from a serious injury, but it was true. She'd have expected he'd have preferred to be away at college, having fun with his friends, but there was no doubt that he was enjoying his convalescence.

The truth was, he and Christian had more in common than he and Tony had ever had, and she couldn't fault Christian's patience with the boy. He encouraged Luis to use his crutches, even helped him down to the beach on one occasion. And they played endless games of chess when it was too hot to go out.

In consequence, the next few days flew by. Because Christian was there to keep Luis company, Olivia had more time for her writing, and her first tale of Dimdum's exploits was almost completed. There were still sketches to do and drawings, but that was the easy part. The story was the thing that had to sell the book.

Of course, she'd had to ring the hospital in San Gimeno and reschedule her appointment. But that was a small price to pay, she told herself, if Luis was happy. Although Christian disturbed her sleep sometimes, she was feeling better, too. Even so, it had been so much easier to convince herself she was doing the right thing by not telling him about the baby when she could dismiss him from her thoughts.

Now it was not so easy. And when he was being nice to her, she sometimes found herself speculating on how he would react if he knew. But whenever she weakened, she reminded herself of the life she had had with Tony. She couldn't accept that kind of marriage again. Not even to give her baby his father's name.

Mealtimes were probably the most difficult. She could evade breakfast. Susannah was more than willing to have her join her in the kitchen for toast and coffee. But lunch and supper were different. Helen usually joined them, for one thing, which made it a more sociable occasion. But it wasn't always easy to enjoy her food with Christian looking on.

It wasn't that he said or did anything outrageous. Or that he always addressed his remarks to her. Indeed, there were times when he was talking to Helen that she felt an unwelcome twinge of resentment. It wasn't that she was jealous, she told herself. It was just a woman's natural pique at being ignored.

Helen, of course, blossomed under his attention. Instead of wearing her uniform, she started dressing much more casually for the evening meal. And she was a pretty girl, with her chestnut curls and slim attractive figure. She made Olivia feel fat and middle-aged and she was sure Christian must notice the difference between them.

The fact that it should matter was just one more reason to feel on edge.

Happily, for Helen, she acquired another admirer. Jules, who had always enjoyed her company, asked her to go with him to a barbecue in town. Perhaps he thought he might have some competition now that Christian was staying at the villa. Whatever, he made his move and Helen accepted his invitation.

As always, the evening of the barbecue was warm and languid. Even the faint breeze that had been around during daylight hours faded with the onset of darkness. It was a perfect night for a barbecue. A perfect night for almost anything except going to bed.

Olivia, who had left her windows open while she had supper, regretted doing so now. Her room felt overly warm and stuffy and she decided to take a walk in the hope that it would cool down.

Leaving her sandals behind, she stepped out onto the veranda. Then, turning away from the front of the building, she padded round to the steps at the back of the villa. Christian and Luis were playing back-gammon on the front terrace and she didn't want to disturb them. Or acquire an unwelcome escort, she reflected wryly. It was much easier if she and Christian didn't spend any time alone.

She trod across the grass soundlessly, the exotic fragrance of the flowers giving the night a sensual appeal. She paused beside a magnolia bush, the creamy white blooms gleaming in the darkness. Its petals felt cool and waxy when she touched them, and they were so flawless in appearance that they almost looked unreal.

As she circled the house she heard the sound of the men's voices drifting towards her. She couldn't hear what they were saying, but they seemed to be enjoying their game. Christian had bought the board game

on one of his trips into town in the pink buggy. It
didn't seem to bother him that it was an unsuitable
vehicle for him to drive.

She reached the beach without incident, heading for
the damp sand that was so much easier to walk on.
The rippling tide covered her toes, cooling and inviting. She wished she dared strip off her clothes and
go skinny-dipping as Christian had done. But, in her
present condition, that wasn't an option.

She contented herself with walking along the
shoreline, stopping every now and then to examine
shells illuminated by the crescent moon. She had no
fear of being alone. San Gimeno was a friendly island.
Unlike on the mainland, crime wasn't a big problem
here.

Which was why she nearly jumped out of her skin
when she turned back and saw the dark figure who
had been following her. Predictably, the moon slipped
behind a cloud at that moment so she had no chance
of seeing who it was. 'Um—Christian?' she ventured
bravely, hoping that whoever it was would assume
she was waiting for someone. Then, her knees almost
buckled beneath her when he answered, 'Yeah, it's
me. Are you crazy coming out here on your own?'

Reaction left her feeling weak and angry. What did
he think he was doing, scaring her like that? Her heart
palpitated in her chest. What right did he have to
question her behaviour? It wasn't the first time she'd
taken a walk on the beach.

Though not at night, a small voice reminded her
mildly. And perhaps she had been a little foolhardy
by not telling anyone where she was going. But the
reason she hadn't told anyone was because she hadn't
wanted this to happen. Even if she had been over-

whelmingly relieved when he'd identified himself just now.

The fact that the situation wouldn't have arisen at all if he hadn't chosen to follow her wasn't worth pursuing, she decided. Summoning her least argumentative tone, she said, 'As a matter of fact, I was on my way back.'

Christian continued towards her, his dark face still unfriendly in the gathering light. The clouds had cleared the moon now and the beach was palely illuminated. 'You should have more sense than walking alone after dark,' he stated grimly. 'I know you don't want my company but it's better than risking being attacked.'

Olivia took a steadying breath as he halted just an arm's-length from her. 'I think you're exaggerating,' she said with apparent calmness. 'In any case, how did you know I was out here? I thought you and Luis were enjoying your game.'

'The game's over,' said Christian flatly. 'And I didn't know you were out here. Not until I saw you.'

'I see.' It was a relief to know he hadn't been following her after all. 'Well—thanks for your concern, but it wasn't necessary. As you can see, we're the only two people on the beach.'

Christian glanced carelessly behind him. 'They're probably all at the barbecue,' he said, and she realised he, too, was trying to be polite. 'Can I walk back with you, or will I be threatening your independence?'

Olivia hesitated, and then she said firmly, 'You've never threatened my independence. My patience perhaps, but I think we've come to an understanding now.' She paused, and when he said nothing she continued quickly, 'And I wanted to thank you for spending so much time with Luis. His father never had a lot of time for him and it's good to see him interacting with an older man for a change.'

'As opposed to an older woman?' suggested Christian drily, and Olivia was glad he couldn't see the sudden colour that entered her cheeks at his words. He waited a beat. 'It occurs to me that you might appreciate a similar situation. I know for a fact that Tony was hardly ever around.'

Olivia rescued her stunned expression. 'Except that you're not older than me,' she said, choosing not to challenge the rest of his statement. 'I appreciate your consideration, but I don't mind being on my own. I've got used to it and—and frankly, you're not my type.'

'So what is your type?' he asked, falling into step beside her as she started back towards the villa. 'Do you think you know me well enough to judge?'

'I know you're like Tony,' she said, stung into an honest answer. 'A woman will always come second to your career.'

Christian smothered an expletive. 'You don't know that.'

'Don't I?' Olivia permitted herself a swift glance in his direction and surprised a look of frustration on his dark face. 'I know Tony only had to crook his finger and you'd do what he wanted. No matter what woman you were with at the time.'

'It doesn't occur to you that that might say more about the woman I was with than my doubtful character?' he demanded angrily. 'Remember, I've never been married. Which is a significant difference between me and Tony, you must admit.'

Olivia shrugged. 'Marriage isn't as important these days.'

'It is to me,' he retorted. 'I consider it very important. Which is why I'd never have married someone like Tony, as you did.'

Olivia came to a standstill. 'I beg your pardon?' Her throat was dry as she stared at him, and the weakness had returned to her legs. 'If you're implying I married Tony for his money—'

'I didn't say that.'

'You implied it,' she insisted, wrapping her arms about her waist. The baby moved, and she caught her breath uneasily. 'You may not believe me, but I loved Tony when I married him. I wanted us to be a real family. Unfortunately that wasn't his intention at all.'

Christian's jaw compressed. 'How could you think it was?'

'Because I was gullible, stupid, call it what you will.' Olivia saw the doubt in his face and knew she had to dispel it. 'I didn't know Tony had had a vasectomy when Luis was just a baby.'

He caught his breath. 'No.'

'Yes.' She swallowed, and, turning away from him, started moving again. 'He married me to give Luis a mother. Nothing more.'

'*Dios*, Olivia—'

His shocked exclamation was heartening. At least he sounded as if he believed her now, she thought. If he doubted it there was no way she could prove it. But what good did it do her admitting how hollow her marriage had been? Was she so desperate for Christian's approval that she'd say anything to justify her actions?

'I had no idea,' he said now, coming up behind

her. And, when she didn't stop, he slipped his arms about her waist and halted her advance. *'Querida,'* he said persuasively in the moment before his hands discovered the distinct swell of her stomach. And then, *'Caramba!'* as he felt the tremor that rippled over the taut muscles at his touch.

Olivia tore herself away from him, a feat that was only possible because for a moment he was too dazed to stop her. But it was too late to hide her secret. She saw the dawning realisation in his face. Before she could spin away from him, his hand shot out and grabbed her wrist.

'You're pregnant,' he said in a stunned voice. Then, his expression changing. *'Madre de Dios*, Olivia, you're having a baby!'

Olivia stared at him helplessly, a hundred reasons why she should deny it coming and going in her head. But before she could voice any of them he spoke again, this time his voice colder, harder. *'Por Dios*, when were you going to tell me this?'

Olivia lifted her shoulders. And then, realising there was no point in trying to deny it, she said carelessly, 'Why should I tell you? You're not my husband.'

'But I am the father of your child,' he snapped, his dark brows almost meeting above his harsh aquiline features. 'Were you hoping I wouldn't find out?'

Olivia's shoulders sagged. It was useless to pretend the baby was Tony's. She'd just burned that particular bridge in her desire to defend herself. 'It's not your problem,' she insisted. 'I'm quite capable of looking after my own child. Now, please—I'd like to go back to the villa.'

'I bet you would.' But there was no sympathy in

Christian's voice. 'You're not going anywhere until you give me an explanation.' He was obviously trying to control his temper, but his lack of success was evident in the clamp he had on her wrist. 'Now—' he sucked in a breath '—I'm willing to accept that it must have been quite a shock for you to discover you were pregnant. It's a shock for me, too, believe me. But that doesn't explain why I wasn't informed of the situation.'

Olivia choked. '"Informed of the situation,"' she mimicked him unsteadily. 'My God, you make it sound like a business deal.'

'Yeah, well, like you say, I'm more used to dealing with business scams than personal ones.'

Olivia gasped. 'This isn't a scam!'

'No?' Christian's dark face was harsh with contempt. 'But you can't deny that this was why you decided you needed to get away on your own for a while. What were you going to do, Olivia? Have the baby and then find some convenient couple to adopt it?'

'No!' Olivia was horrified. 'I wouldn't do that!'

'Why not? It's obviously an inconvenience for you.'

She stared at him. 'Why do you say that?'

'Because if it wasn't you wouldn't be hiding away here, on San Gimeno. You don't want anyone to know about it because you don't intend to keep it.' His fingers tightened painfully. 'Did you try to get rid of it?'

'No!' Olivia felt sickened at the thought. 'How could you ask such a thing?'

'Okay.' He seemed to accept that and she was absurdly grateful. 'So why run away?'

'I didn't run away.' But she had and, deciding he deserved at least a part of the truth, she went on, 'I— I just wanted to have the baby before anyone found out about it. That's all.'

'Why?'

'What do you mean?'

'Why was it so important for you to have had the baby before you told anyone else?'

Oh, God!

How was she supposed to answer that without him guessing the truth?

'Look,' she said earnestly, 'Tony had just died. What would people have thought if I'd suddenly announced I was pregnant?'

Christian shrugged. 'They'd have thought it was his,' he said flatly. 'A reasonable assumption, don't you think?'

Olivia shook her head. 'Perhaps.'

'Why perhaps? No one knew about Tony's vasectomy, did they?'

'Well, no...'

Christian's brows arched in silent enquiry and she sighed before going on. 'I—I didn't think it was something Luis needed to know about. He has enough to contend with right now.'

'Luis!' Christian was scornful now. 'I think you mean me, don't you, *querida*? It was me you ran away from; me you didn't want to tell. Were you afraid I wouldn't believe it was mine?'

'No.'

'Why, then?'

'Oh—' Deciding there was no point in avoiding it any longer, Olivia gave in. 'If you must know, I didn't want you to know about the baby, period. It was a mistake. It never should have happened. The responsibility for what happens now is mine.' Her jaw bunched. 'Does that satisfy you?'

The silence that fell after this outburst was hardly comfortable. The tension was almost palpable, the air spiked with the anger she was sure her words would provoke.

But Christian didn't respond as she expected. Instead of accusing her of lying to him, he looked down at his hand curled about her wrist. Brown skin against white, just a trace of redness revealing the pressure he was exerting. Then, almost imperceptibly, his hold slackened to allow his thumb to massage the veins on the inner side of her arm.

Olivia was too bemused to stop him. The pad of his thumb rubbed insistently over the sensitive skin, creating an explosive heat every place he touched. When, with a faint twisting of his lips, he brought her wrist to his mouth and put his tongue to the wildly palpitating pulse he found here, she could only stand and stare.

Then he lifted his head and looked at her. 'Does it satisfy me?' he asked, and for a moment she hadn't the first idea what he was talking about. 'Did you really expect it would?'

Sanity returned with a rush. 'I thought you would understand my feelings,' she said swiftly. 'You guessed why I left Miami, and I've explained how I feel. I want this baby. I do. But I don't want—I don't *need* anything from you.'

Christian's nostrils flared with sudden impatience and as if it offended him to touch her now, he let her go. '*Dios*, Olivia, you must see this changes everything.'

'No. Why should it?' She refused to allow the thought that this was what she'd been afraid of all along. 'You have your own life, your own friends, your own career. You don't want the complication of a baby upsetting your regime, making demands on your time. I appreciate your concerns and—and in other circumstances—'

'What other circumstances?'

'Well—' She searched wildly for an answer. 'If—if you and I had been having a relationship, for example. If we'd been seeing one another for some time and this had happened. Even if we'd split up, I could understand—'

'*Basta!*' Enough! His harsh interjection cut her off, his face darkening now with the anger she had anticipated earlier. 'Sometimes I am convinced you will never understand me, *querida*.' He used the endearment deliberately, she thought, but there was no trace of affection in the word. 'I am not interested in the pathetic excuses you give for keeping this from me. I am the child's father. I deserved to know. It takes two people to make a baby, Olivia. I think you have forgotten that.'

'I haven't forgotten anything,' she mumbled resentfully. She hated it that he was treating her as if she were incapable of intelligent thought. 'You just don't understand—'

'No.' He was bitter. 'I don't. I don't know how you could think that now I know about the baby I might be willing to walk away and forget all about it.' He gave a short, mirthless laugh. '*Dios*, what am I? A monster?'

'I never said you were a monster,' protested Olivia urgently. 'And I would never think such a thing.'

'Then why—'

'This isn't about you,' she exclaimed wearily. 'It's about me. Like I said before, I want this baby.' She ran an involuntary hand over her stomach and then withdrew it awkwardly. 'I—I want it desperately. But I don't want to be a part of any man's life ever again.'

She heard Christian suck in a breath and prepared to defend herself. But all he said was, 'This is about Tony, of course.'

She saw no reason to deny it. 'Yes.'

'You don't want another marriage like the one you had with Tony?'

Marriage?

She was too shocked to say anything but, 'No.'

'No.' Christian acknowledged her response evenly, running a hand round the back of his neck as he spoke. 'But not all men are like my cousin,' he went on as her eyes were drawn to the dark hair exposed by his gaping shirt. 'Some men actually honour their marriage vows.'

Olivia dragged her eyes away and made a dismissive gesture. If he expected an argument from her, he would wait a long time. She didn't know where this was going but she suspected she wasn't going to like it. The last thing she wanted was for him to feel he had to make any sacrifices for her.

There was silence for a few moments and she was on the point of saying that they ought to be getting back when Christian said softly, 'And Luis doesn't know?'

Olivia sighed. 'You know he doesn't.'

'Good.' Christian brought his hand over his head, rumpling his hair as he did so. 'That's good. That makes things easier. Much easier.'

'Makes what easier?' asked Olivia warily, wishing he weren't so attractive. Everything he did, every move he made, seemed designed to provoke her interest. Even now, with his hair sticking out at odd angles, he was disturbingly male, disturbingly appealing. 'I don't know what you're talking about.'

Christian's mouth softened. 'I'm talking about us, *querida*. I'm talking about the fact that you are pregnant and Luis is of the opinion that you and I dislike one another.'

Olivia swallowed uneasily. 'So?'

'So he will not suspect anything like this when we announce our engagement.'

'What?'

Olivia was horrified but Christian seemed indifferent to her dismay. 'I said—'

'I know what you said,' she interrupted him fiercely. 'But you're crazy if you think I'm going to let you tell Luis that we're getting engaged. No! No way. I wouldn't marry you if—if—'

'If I was the last man on earth?' he suggested mildly. 'I believe that is the metaphor you are looking for. And I won't insult your intelligence by making the obvious retort.' He paused. 'But you will marry me, Olivia. You will give my child my name. It is what I want; what I demand.'

'You demand?' She almost choked on the words. 'You can't demand that I do anything.'

'Perhaps not.' His voice was tight. 'But in my family, we have honour, Olivia. We have integrity. We do not neglect our responsibilities.'

Olivia made an aggravated sound. 'I keep telling you, this is not your responsibility.'

'I disagree.'

She shook her head helplessly. 'You can't make me marry you,' she insisted. 'I won't do it.'

Christian sighed then. 'Why?' he asked flatly. 'You say you don't hate me. *Bien.* So—am I so very repugnant to you that you cannot countenance our living together, even for the sake of the child?'

Olivia groaned. 'You're not repugnant to me, Christian. You know that. You're only trying reverse psychology to make me feel bad.'

'Am I?' Dark lashes shadowed his eyes. 'Yet you are telling me you would rather bear this burden alone than allow me to care for you?'

Olivia shook her head. 'You don't care for me.'

'How do you know?'

'Because you don't.' She took a breath and then continued doggedly, 'Any more than I care for you.' And, oh, God, she wished that were true! 'Christian, please, let me do this my way.'

'And what if I tell you I do care about you?' he persisted, putting out his hand and allowing his fingertips to graze the curve of her chin. 'I do, you know. For my sins.'

'You don't!' She was horrified at the way her heart leapt at his words. She knew why he was saying it, of course. Demanding that she obey him hadn't worked, so he was trying persuasion. 'And I don't appreciate your lying to me to try and get your own way.'

A pained look crossed his face. 'Isn't that what you've been doing?' he asked bitterly. Then, '*En todo caso*—in any case, you're wrong. Why do you think I came to the island? Why do you think I wanted to stay? Because I wanted us to get to know one another better. Because I hoped that you might begin to believe that what happened the night Tony died was meant to be.'

'No—'

'Yes.' Christian's hand trailed from her face down her neck to the sensual slope of her breasts. His thumb flicked a swollen nipple and she drew back in alarm. 'And whatever you say, I still think we could be happy together.'

'No.' Olivia couldn't let him go on. 'What you're talking about isn't about us. It's about you—and the baby.'

'So?'

'So—do you honestly think I'd accept that kind of a relationship?' she cried incredulously. 'My God, you sound just like Tony! That's what he said. That we could be happy together, him and Luis and me. And look how that turned out!'

'I'm not Tony.'

'No, you're not. But you're like him. You give ultimatums; you make demands. You think that just because I'm having your baby that gives you some rights over me. It doesn't. I've made a life for myself. I don't need you or anyone else.'

'*Por Dios*, Olivia—'

'No.' She held up her hand to silence him. 'Don't say anything more. You've said enough. And if you think I would marry you just to give my baby a name, you're very much mistaken. I've had one marriage where my husband thought that so long as he supported me financially, he could do what the hell he liked—and with whom. You must be crazy if you think I'd go through that again.'

Christian's aquiline features looked frozen now. 'I keep telling you, I am not like Tony,' he grated harshly. 'Do you think I would do that to a woman I professed to love?'

To love?

For a moment Olivia was tempted to stop and explore that statement, but disbelief and her own common sense drove her on.

'I don't know what you'd do,' she admitted honestly. 'But I'm not prepared to take that risk. And— and if you do care about me at all, you'll go away and let me get on with my life.'

'And Luis?'

Her heart slumped uncertainly. Dear God, surely he wasn't going to hold Luis's ignorance of her condition over her.

'I—I'll tell Luis, when the time is right,' she appended hurriedly, turning away, unable to face him any longer. 'Please, Christian. You've got to let me do this my way.'

CHAPTER TEN

Luis returned to California six weeks later.

For the last couple of weeks before he left, he'd been agitating to go, and finally Dr Hoffman had given his consent. Luis still had problems getting around, of course. He needed the aid of a cane. But he'd convinced both Olivia and Christian that he'd be happier getting on with his life. He'd wasted enough time as it was.

Despite the misgivings Olivia had had when Luis had come to stay with her, she was sorry to see him go. She was glad he was so much better. That went without saying. And it would mean she no longer had to hide her condition. But she'd got used to having him around, got used to his company. She'd even begun to depend on him, she admitted, when she was feeling particularly low.

Also, so long as Luis was there, there was always the chance that Christian might return to the island. Although she'd assured herself she was relieved when he'd left, lately she'd begun to regret the way she'd behaved. She'd even found herself wondering if she'd been too hasty in rejecting his proposal. She couldn't deny she cared about him and that was the truth. Would it have required such a leap of faith to hope he might come to care about her? It seemed she was never to know.

He had respected her wishes and not told Luis about her pregnancy. She wanted to tell her stepson in her own good time. If he'd had any suspicions, she would have had to tell him. But Luis was too involved with his own recovery. It could wait, she told herself, at least until the baby was born.

Thinking about Christian was not wise, however, and she always rejected any weakening on her part. She only had to remind herself of the life she'd lived with Tony to assure herself that she couldn't risk it happening again. And it would be so much worse this time. She'd never loved Tony as she loved Christian.

Nevertheless, it was a painful situation. And while she kept telling herself that she was perfectly capable of having this baby on her own, some troubling thoughts did intrude. Would it be fair to deny Christian the right to share in his child's upbringing? she wondered. How long did she intend to keep the child's identity a secret?

Confiding in Susannah had become necessary. The housekeeper had already guessed her mistress was pregnant and she'd agreed to keep Olivia's condition to herself.

'It'll be good for you to have some company,' she remarked, after Luis had departed. 'I just wish my daughter had wanted a family instead of filling her head with all that education.'

Susannah was a widow, Olivia knew, and her only daughter was a professor of history at a university in Chicago. Susannah was proud of her, of course, but she missed having her family around her. Olivia hoped that when the baby was born the woman would find some compensation in helping her look after her child instead.

Luis's leaving also signalled the completion of her first manuscript. After printing it out on the computer she'd installed in the spare room, she viewed the sheaf of pages with real pride. She'd done it, she thought. She'd finished her first book. Now all it needed was for Dimdum's antics to touch some over-worked editor's heart.

Wanting an unbiased viewpoint, she let Susannah read the manuscript before she posted it. The house-keeper seemed enthusiastic, but Olivia couldn't help wondering if she was only saying what she wanted to hear. Her drawings, the ones she'd so painstakingly painted in watercolours, couldn't be copied to her satisfaction, so she took a chance and enclosed the originals with the book.

However, two weeks after she'd despatched the manuscript, something happened to put its acceptance or otherwise out of her head. On one of her regular visits to the hospital in San Gimeno she learned that the baby had turned into the breech position, with its feet facing the birth passage instead of up under her ribs.

It was possible it might turn again, the doctor told her reassuringly, but if not she might be forced to have a Caesarean delivery. And while Olivia tried not to worry, she couldn't deny she was anxious. With only Susannah to confide in, she had never felt so alone.

It was just more proof that there were disadvantages to having this baby in secret. She'd already born the embarrassment of not having anyone to help her with her breathing exercises and that had been hard. Sharing the classes with couples who were so obviously in love had brought the truth home to her, and now, facing an uncertain delivery in San Gimeno's small hospital, she wondered if she was really as in-dependent as she'd thought.

But there was no question of contacting Christian. She'd destroyed any affection he might have felt for her by sending him away. She had to face the fact that she had only herself to blame and get on with it. She wasn't a child. She didn't need anybody to hold her hand.

Then, about five weeks before the baby was due, Christian phoned.

Olivia answered the call herself, expecting it to be Luis. Her stepson had phoned every week since his return to Berkeley, just to let her know he was doing okay, and she was taken aback when she heard Christian's accented tones.

'Olivia?'

She swallowed. 'Who else?' she answered, glad of the arm of the sofa behind her. Her legs felt decidedly shaky and she couldn't make up her mind whether she was pleased or sorry. Pleased, because she'd so much longed to hear his voice, and sorry, because speaking to him reminded her painfully of what she could never have.

'How are you?' he asked, and there was genuine concern in his voice, a fact that stupidly brought the hot tears to her eyes.

'I—I'm okay,' she said, making a decision not to tell him about the baby's position. 'Um—a bit tired, perhaps. But that's natural in the circumstances.'

'You're not overdoing it?'

'Overdoing what?' Olivia tried to sound amused. 'I'm hardly run off my feet, Christian. Luis left weeks ago.'

'I know that.'

'You've spoken to him?' Of course he had. Luis was bound to have kept Christian updated about his whereabouts.

But something of her concern must have shown in her voice because he said flatly, 'I haven't told him any secrets, if that's what you're afraid of.'

'Good.'

She wondered if she meant it. It was such a relief to speak to someone who knew.

'Anyway, I meant I hope you're not overdoing your writing and so on,' he continued. 'Concentrating is tiring. I know that.'

'Oh, I'm not writing at the moment.' She was pleased to have something positive to tell him. 'I finished my book just after Luis went back to California. It's with a publisher as we speak.'

'It's been accepted?'

He sounded impressed and she wished she didn't have to admit she hadn't heard a word since it had been despatched. 'Not yet,' she said with deliberate optimism. 'But I'm living in hope.'

'I see.' Christian hesitated. 'You decided not to let an agent look at it first?'

'No.' She could hardly tell him that she'd hardly thought about the book in weeks. 'I don't know any agents anyway.'

'I do.'

'Oh, right.' Olivia was sardonic. 'And you'd have been willing to help me after the way I behaved when you offered your assistance before?'

'I don't bear grudges,' retorted Christian softly, and Olivia felt a desperate urge to test that submission. It would be so nice to have him on her side.

Expelling an unsteady breath, she pushed such unworthy thoughts aside and said carefully, 'So—how are things with you? How's Julie? Still as mad about you as ever, I suppose.'

'I doubt it.' Christian was dismissive. 'I haven't seen Julie in months. We split up the week before I came to San Gimeno.'

'Ah.'

'What's that supposed to mean?'

'Nothing.' Olivia refused to admit that it explained his sudden arrival on the island. 'So—who has taken her place? Anyone I know?'

'Stop treating me like a schoolboy, Olivia.' His voice had hardened now. 'I'm not a child. I don't need a stream of women to assert my masculinity as Tony did.'

Olivia quivered. 'I'm sorry.'

'No, dammit, you're not.' He spoke harshly. 'But instead of assuming that the reason I came to San Gimeno was because I'd split up with Julie, you should consider the alternative. That I split up with Julie because I wanted to see you.'

Olivia smoothed a moist palm over the seam of her shorts, realising she should have known better than to think he wouldn't detect her evasion. 'I don't think that's very likely,' she demurred, even though her heart skipped a beat at the thought. 'But thank you for saying it.'

'Why is it so hard for you to believe that I might mean what I say?' he demanded savagely. 'Dammit, Olivia, until I found out about the baby, I thought you were beginning to like me, to trust me. What did I do wrong?'

'You didn't do anything wrong.' She drew a trembling breath. 'And I do like you, Christian. But you know you and I would never—work.'

'Because I'm Tony's cousin.' He spoke flatly.

'We're not compatible,' she insisted. 'Apart from anything else, I'm older than you are and—'

'Ah.' He snorted. 'I wondered when you'd bring that up.'

'Well, it's true,' she said. 'You can't deny it. But mostly it's because I'd always know you only asked me to marry you because of the baby. *Your* baby. I'm flattered that you'd be prepared to make the sacrifice, but that doesn't stop me seeing the flaws.'

'All I see is you dredging up reasons not to be honest with me,' he said bitterly. 'All right. Maybe my proposal was premature, but that doesn't mean it wasn't sincere.'

'I believe you.' And she did. 'But I am being honest with you. Surely you can see that I'm telling you the truth?'

'I don't think you're ever going to forgive me for taking advantage of you,' he told her wearily. 'By making love to you the night Tony died, you believe I proved what you've always thought: that I'm no better than he was.'

He rang off then before she could respond and, although she told herself that was all to the good, she couldn't help wishing she had had the time to explain how she felt. In truth, she didn't blame Christian; she blamed herself for what had happened. And it was too late now to wonder what might have been if they hadn't given in to that desperate urge of sexual need.

The call came in the early hours of the morning. Christian, who hadn't slept well in weeks, had just swallowed half a bottle of single malt and lost consciousness when the phone beside his bed awakened him.

Cursing, he reached for the receiver with an unsteady hand, in no mood to deal with someone else's problems at the moment. 'Yeah,' he said harshly, daring whoever was on the other end to challenge him, and then swore again when the line went dead.

Slamming the handset onto its cradle, he sank back against his pillows, resting his forearm against his temple in weary resignation. Exactly what he needed, he thought. An anonymous caller. What kind of person got off on calling unsuspecting strangers in the middle of the night?

His attempt at sleep ruined, half an hour later he switched on the lights and got up, walking over to the curtained windows of his apartment and peering out. The gardens around the exclusive complex were deserted. Even the ever-present security guard had evidently taken a breather from the heat.

Unwillingly, he found himself wondering what the weather was like on San Gimeno. When he'd spoken to Olivia a couple of days ago, he hadn't thought to ask. Pretty hot, he guessed. Pretty tiring, too, for someone in her condition. He wished he could do something to help her, but she wanted nothing from him.

Until he'd rung her himself, he'd kept up with how she was via Luis. It had been easy to slip in a question about Olivia when he was speaking to the younger man. Not that Luis could tell him anything of significance, but at least he'd have heard if something had gone wrong. Luis still thought he harboured some animosity towards her and it had offered too much of a challenge to persuade him otherwise.

Now, he turned away from the windows, wondering again who had called him. The suspicion that Luis might be in more trouble was foremost in his mind. It could be Dolores Samuels, of course. She'd been peeved when he'd had her transferred out of state. But he couldn't stand her constant jibes about Olivia, and he knew that sooner or later he'd have told her the truth.

Which was? He scowled. That he was in love with Olivia? Or that she was expecting his child and not being with her was driving him mad? Both of the above, he thought, wondering how he was ever going to convince Olivia he meant it. It was a bitter irony that the only woman he really cared about only saw him as a facsimile of her late husband, something that up until now he'd wanted to be.

His shoulders sagged. It was no use trying to change her mind at the moment. She was bound and determined to have this baby without anyone's help and it was up to him not to cause her any more stress than she already had. But after the baby was born, she might be more willing to listen to reason. Though he wasn't holding out any hopes. Not until she'd got the image of him as Tony out of her mind.

He had thought of trying to find out where she'd sent her manuscript. But he knew she wouldn't thank him, if he interfered. He had to accept the situation as it was and get over it. At least until the baby was born.

With this thought in mind, he eventually managed to get back to sleep again. But he was up at six, taking a shower, trying to get his mind back on track. He was spending too much time thinking about Olivia. And about how she'd feel if he made another un-scheduled visit to the island...

When Luis rang at eight-thirty he was already in his office at the Mora Building, drinking his ump-teenth cup of coffee and trying to make some sense of the current crop of economic statistics. With half the world in a recession, the Mora Corporation had to keep ahead of the game.

The phone shrilled beside him and he reached for the receiver almost gratefully. 'Rodrigues,' he said, expecting the caller to be on the other side of the world. But instead of the world, it was the other side of the country. And, glancing at his watch, Christian felt the same apprehension he'd felt in the middle of the night.

'Luis?' he said, in answer to the young man's breathless greeting. '*Muy Dios*, since when do you get up at five in the morning?'

'Since I got word that Mom's in the hospital,' re-torted Luis, without hesitation. 'Dammit, Chris, did you know she was expecting a baby?'

Christian's stomach plunged and the numerous cups of coffee he'd consumed rose sickly into his throat. 'I—how did you find that out?' he stumbled, not sure how to answer him. Dear God, he should have realised the hospital would contact Luis. He was no doubt nominated as her next of kin.

'They phoned me,' Luis answered now, apparently not detecting Christian's uncertainty. 'They tried to get me last night, but—well, I didn't spend the night in my own room.' He broke off and Christian heard what sounded suspiciously like a sob in his voice.

'God, she should have told me, Chris. I'd have been there for her. You know I would.'

Christian was still trying to get his head round the fact that someone had phoned Luis hours ago. Holy Mother, was that who had tried to ring him, too?

'Is she all right?' he asked, his brain snapping into action finally. 'You say she's in the hospital. I—has she had the baby?' Surely it hadn't been due for several more weeks?

Luis sniffed again. 'I think she's going to be all right,' he mumbled a little uncertainly, and Christian had to force back the words he wanted to say. Like, *you must know, Luis. You've probably spoken to her doctor. Por Dios,* didn't he realise how frustrating this was?

Of course, he didn't. He couldn't. Olivia's independence had put them all in a difficult position. His heart ached at the thought that there might have been a problem. He should have been with her, he thought. She should have been able to depend on him.

'Luis!'

The boy wasn't saying anything and Christian couldn't hide his impatience. The longer Luis delayed, the more apprehensive Christian grew. He tried to think. By his reckoning the baby hadn't been due for another month. Was that normal? He wished he'd paid more attention to biology lessons at school.

'She should have told me,' repeated Luis again, and Christian realised the boy was in a state of shock. 'All those weeks we were together and she never said a word about it. Like, as if I'd have had her running after me if I'd known she was pregnant.'

'It doesn't matter now, Luis,' said Christian, controlling himself manfully. 'Tell me what happened last night. Is Olivia okay?'

'I think so.' Once again Luis was ambivalent. 'You know, I never intended to go to Marvin's party. But all the gang were going and—'

'Luis, I'm not interested in where you spent the night.' Christian was almost at the end of his tether and the strain was beginning to show in his voice. 'Who called you? When did they call you? What for God's sake did they say?'

'Hey, there's no need to take that tone with me, man.' Luis had sobered now, and Christian realised he was in danger of losing the only ally he had. 'The doctor phoned. I don't know what time it was. Probably about midnight, I think. I can't be certain. Then he called again just now as I was coming in.'

'Okay.' Christian's nails dug into his palms as he tried to calm himself. 'So—she's had the baby, yeah? That's what he called about?'

'Was it?' Luis broke off. Then, 'You knew, didn't you? That's why you're so—cool about it.' *Cool!* 'Why did she tell you and not me?'

Christian's eyes closed. 'Does it matter?' he asked. 'Just tell me what the doctor said.'

'It's yours, isn't it?' Luis continued, ignoring the other man's urgency. 'My God, how long have you been screwing my mother? Did it start before Dad bought the farm?'

'No!' Christian couldn't keep the agony out of his voice. 'No, it didn't,' he said. 'And I've not been— screwing your mother, as you so charmingly put it. I made love to her once. Only once. And this is the result.'

Luis sounded sullen now. 'Why should I believe you?'

'Because I've never lied to you,' said Christian wearily. 'In the circumstances, why the hell should I start now?'

Luis sniffed. 'That doesn't alter the fact that I should have been told she was having a baby,' he persisted. 'I'm her son. Why would she want to keep it from me?'

'She wanted to keep it from everyone.' Christian spoke tiredly. 'I only found out because—well, I did.' He took a breath and then added flatly, 'I guess I've had more experience with these things than you.'

'You're sure you weren't—you know, doing it while you were staying at the villa?'

'No!' Christian was adamant. 'I told you what happened and it's the truth.'

'So that's why you always acted so hostile towards one another,' Luis considered thoughtfully. 'I'm guessing that Mom regretted what had happened.' He paused. 'Did you?'

'No.' Christian wanted to yell in frustration. 'Luis, can't we discuss this later when we've got more time to talk about it? When you've told me what happened to Olivia last night?'

'I guess.' But Luis seemed in no hurry now to reassure him. 'But how do I know that Mom would want me talking to you?'

'Luis!'

At last Christian's anger seemed to get through to his cousin, and with a careless grunt, he said, 'Yeah, it was a pity about the baby. It was a—a premature birth, I think that was what the doctor said. They had been intending to do a C-section. But Mom went into labour and they had to take the baby any way they could.'

Christian stifled a groan. It didn't sound good, but right now he couldn't worry about the baby. 'Olivia,' he said desperately. 'Is Olivia all right?'

'Like I said before, I think so. But the doctor says she's lost a lot of blood. That's why they phoned me. Like, I'm her next of kin, you know? I got the impression it was touch and go for a time.'

Dios!

Christian didn't know how he controlled his temper. The anger springing inside him was hot and painful and violently real. He wanted to strangle Luis for bleating on about what Olivia should or shouldn't have told him. She had lost a lot of blood. She may have lost the baby. He had to get to San Gimeno at once.

'You okay?' Luis asked suddenly, as if aware that Christian had fallen silent now, and he forced himself to make a suitable response.

'Yeah,' he said, his mind still reeling. 'But I've got to see her, Luis. I'll speak to you later, after I find out what's going on.'

'Hey, I'm coming, too, man,' protested Luis immediately. 'Just as soon as I can get on a flight.'

'Well, I'll meet you there,' said Christian, having no intention of waiting for him to get to Miami. 'Take care, I'll probably see you later on.'

'Wait.'

As he would have hung up Luis's cry stopped him. 'What is it?' he said, not prepared to indulge in any more argument right now.

'Why are you going to see her?' asked Luis. 'If

you and Mom were just a one-time thing, why do you need to see her now?'

Christian sighed then. 'Because I love her,' he said simply. 'It may be hard for you to believe, but I can't imagine living the rest of my life without her. But you're right, too, she doesn't care about me. That's why she wanted to keep me out. But, forgive me, I can't worry about her reaction at this moment. I'll do anything she wants, go anywhere she says, but, please God, just let her be all right.'

CHAPTER ELEVEN

OLIVIA put a tentative hand beneath the sheet that was all that covered her and was quite surprised to find her stomach wasn't completely flat. For someone who felt as if she'd been run over by a steamroller, she was still far too fat to have had the baby.

But she had. Right now, her daughter was asleep in the hospital's nursery, uncaring that her precipitate arrival had almost cost her mother her life. Of course, she hadn't known that arrangements had been made for her to arrive two weeks from now; that Dr Collins had planned to operate before her mother could go into labour.

Instead, Olivia had found herself alone at the villa when the first pains had gripped her. As luck would have it, she had given Susannah the night off to go to a movie. And, although the housekeeper had offered to stay with her mistress, Olivia had assured her that she still had plenty of time before the baby was due.

That she didn't have plenty of time had become apparent when her waters had broken. With what she'd soon realised were contractions occurring at regular intervals, Olivia had grabbed her bag and stumbled out to the Jeep. Thank God for Christian's forethought, she'd breathed as she'd swung the vehicle round and headed into town. Without the Jeep, she'd have had to rely on a taxi. And at that time of the evening there was no guarantee that one would be available.

She'd considered calling the ambulance, but having a baby wasn't an emergency, she'd assured herself. It was just a little bit frightening when you were on your own. But if she could just get to the hospital, she had great faith in Dr Collins. He would know what to do to get her though this.

In fact, she'd only just made it to the hospital. She'd been in so much pain and concentrating on the road had been almost impossible. By the time she'd staggered into the emergency room she'd been as white as the paint on the walls. But it had been such a relief to be able to relax.

Even so, the rest of the night had become a nightmare. There'd been examinations and more examinations and all the while she'd been forced to withstand the pain. They hadn't wanted to give her any drugs until they knew if Dr Collins was going to operate. But it eventually had become apparent that it would be too dangerous to try a C-section now.

By morning, the pain had become excruciating, and Dr Collins had suggested calling Luis to give her some support. But Olivia had refused. The last thing she'd wanted was to panic her stepson, particularly as he didn't even know she was expecting a baby.

Late afternoon, and Olivia had been totally exhausted. Even the gas and air they'd given her hadn't been keeping the agony at bay. She'd known Dr Collins and the nurses were worried about her. Their faces had convinced her of that. She'd been sure she was going to die, she and her baby, and in a weak moment she'd wished she dared phone Christian and ask him to come.

Then, just when it had seemed that nothing good could happen, the breakthrough had come. With one almighty push, she'd managed to expel the baby's legs from her womb. It had enabled Dr Collins, who she'd guessed must have been as tired as she was, to help her by turning the baby, and seconds later her daughter had come into the world.

She didn't remember much after that, only the moment when they'd put the baby into her arms. She'd been trembling so badly, she could hardly hold her, but she'd seen the baby's dark hair and olive skin and known she was her father's child.

Then the baby had been whisked away so that she could be tended to. Hushed voices had spoken above her bed, but she'd been too bemused to care what they were saying. She'd known she was bleeding, badly. She'd been able to feel it. Yet she'd been so relieved that the pain had gone away that she hadn't realised what the spreading numbness had meant.

It had apparently taken several hours to stabilise her; several hours during which time she had given the doctor permission to call her stepson with the news. She didn't remember doing so; she didn't remember much at all actually. Until Dr Collins had come to see her this morning and told her how lucky she'd been, she hadn't appreciated how close to death she'd come.

But now the sun was shining, she'd just had a lovely cool bath, and she was feeling so much better. A little weak still, but Dr Collins had assured her that that was to be expected in the circumstances. Nevertheless, she was strong enough to wonder what Luis must have thought when he'd heard she'd had a baby. Would he be thinking the worst of her? She hoped not. She and her stepson had always been so close.

And Christian...

But she knew she shouldn't think about Christian now, not while she was feeling so emotional. Anticipating how he would react when he heard he had a daughter was not something she could cope with right now. The trouble was, in her weakened state, she was likely to say or do something stupid. Like hoping he would love the baby—and how pitiful was that?

A shadow darkened the doorway suddenly and she turned her head to see a nurse wheeling a trolley on which rested a phone into her room. Olivia was aware that her heartbeat had quickened, but that was because for a moment she'd hoped it might be Christian. Or Luis, she amended rapidly. But the young man couldn't have made it from San Francisco in so short a time.

'You have a call, Mrs Mora,' said the nurse, bending down to attach the jack. 'Are you up to taking it? It's from your son.'

'Luis...' Olivia felt a momentary anxiety, but then she nodded. She had to speak to him sooner or later and it might be easier to break the news over the phone.

'You're sure you want to talk to him?' The young nurse had picked up on her ambivalence, and Olivia felt ashamed to be so reluctant to speak to her stepson.

'Please,' she said firmly, trying to struggle higher on her pillows, and the nurse came to help her up. Olivia felt foolish being too weak to do such a simple thing without assistance, but the nurse's eyes were kind and she handed her the receiver with a smile.

'I'll be back in a few minutes,' she said. 'Try not to get too excited. It's important to keep your blood pressure under control.'

Olivia would have thought that was impossible at present, but she accepted that the nursing staff knew best. 'I will,' she said, and put the receiver to her ear. She smiled as the nurse left her, then added tentatively, 'Luis? Luis, is that you?'

'Who were you expecting?' Luis asked gruffly, and she couldn't mistake the edge of hostility in his voice. 'Rodrigues, I suppose. He told me he was the baby's father. You and he must have been having some laugh at my expense!'

'No!' Olivia was horrified that he should think such a thing. What had Christian been telling him, for heaven's sake? And how had Christian found out? 'Luis, you know I would never do anything to hurt you. Whatever Christian's said, you can believe that.'

'So why didn't you tell me you were having his baby?' Luis demanded. 'Mom, you must have known how I'd feel hearing the news from someone else. Okay, Chris is cool and I like him. But, dammit, Mom, I deserved to be told the truth.'

'I know.' Olivia acknowledged that she had hurt him. Albeit unwillingly, but that was no excuse. 'I suppose I was too ashamed to admit it. I didn't want you to think badly of me, I suppose.'

'Ashamed?' Luis was taken aback now. 'Hey, Mom, there's no need for you to feel ashamed. I know you had a tough time with my father. What you do with your life now is your affair.' He paused a moment and when he spoke again his voice had gentled. 'I hear you've had a rough few hours. How are you feeling now?'

Olivia expelled a shaky breath. 'I'm—okay,' she said, not wanting to burden him with all the details. 'And—and your baby sister is okay, too, if you're interested.'

'If I'm interested?' Luis gave a snort. 'How about that? I've got a baby sister.' He sounded almost pleased. 'I can't wait to see her. And you, of course.'

'Well, whenever you can get away, we'll be glad to see you,' murmured Olivia, hardly daring to believe that the worst was over. She'd anticipated this moment for so long and now it was almost an anticlimax.

'I'll be there this afternoon,' declared Luis suddenly, startling her back to awareness. 'You can tell Chris when he gets there that I'm taking the eleven o'clock flight.'

'Chris? I mean Christian?' Olivia's mouth had gone dry and she could hardly articulate the words. 'He's coming here?' Oh, God, she didn't want to see him. How on earth was she going to hide her feelings if he showed any kindness to her now?

'Yeah.' Luis spoke again, his words arresting her anxious meanderings. 'The guy's in shock, I think. Be nice to him, Mom. He's feeling pretty devastated because you didn't want him to know, either.'

Olivia was still holding the phone when the nurse came back to check on her. She took the now-dead receiver from Olivia's hand and replaced it on its cradle. Then she said reprovingly, 'What's happened? What did your son say to you, Mrs Mora? I hope he hasn't been upsetting you. You look as pale as a ghost.'

Olivia shook her head. 'I'm all right,' she said,

forcing a smile for the nurse's benefit. And then, more firmly, 'When can I get out of this bed?'

Perhaps she'd feel stronger if she could face Christian on her feet, she thought. More in control of herself, at least. She had to be strong for her daughter's sake. It was important to remember why she'd kept him away.

'Dr Collins will decide when he thinks you're fit enough to get up,' declared the nurse, straightening her pillows and flicking the sheet into place. 'Now, I'm going to leave you to have a rest and then in an hour or so I'll bring your baby to you. You'll need all your strength when the little one needs feeding.'

Olivia's lips trembled at the thought of feeding her daughter. So far, they'd only put the baby to her breast once and it hadn't been a success. But now she was feeling better, she was looking forward to the experience. And to holding her baby again. It seemed so long since she'd had that precious bundle in her arms.

The nurse left and, despite her determination to prepare herself in case Luis was right and Christian did turn up, Olivia's eyes refused to stay open. She'd just doze for a little while, she thought, feeling pleasantly drowsy. The nurse would come to warn her if she had any visitors, wanted or otherwise.

The light touch on her hand was pleasant, too, she thought. She was dreaming and in the dream Christian was standing beside her bed. But it was a dream because there were tears in his eyes and his face looked drawn and haggard in a way she had never seen before. He seemed to be saying something—his lips were moving—but she couldn't hear what it was.

Then the fingers around hers tightened and all illusions that this was just a dream left her. With wide, startled eyes, she gazed up into Christian's dark, tormented face. She hadn't been imagining it. He did look drained and tired. And as she stared at him he released her hand, as if he was afraid she might be offended by his touch.

There was a moment's silence when he raked back his tumbled hair with an unsteady hand, and then he said harshly, *'Gracias a Dios, eres bien!'* Thank God, you're all right!

Olivia's tongue circled her upper lip. 'I—I'm fine,' she said, which wasn't strictly true, but it would suffice. She took a breath. 'There was no need for you to come.'

'Dios, por supuesto—this is, of course I needed to come,' he retorted, and she realised how distracted he must be to speak in his own language instead of hers. *'Dios*, Olivia, I didn't know what to expect after I got Luis's phone call. He seemed to think it was a matter of life and death!'

Olivia shook her head. 'You know how melodramatic Luis can be,' she said, concentrating on her hands, which were almost as pale as the sheet. It saved her from looking at Christian, from noticing with greedy eyes that, even distraught as he was, he was still achingly attractive. Oh, God, she wished she'd had more time to prepare for this. She was in danger of believing anything he said.

'No obstante, nevertheless,' he said now unevenly, dropping down onto his haunches beside the bed, 'you should have let me know if there was a problem. You have no idea how helpless I felt when Luis told me what happened last night.' He took a breath. 'I wanted to be with you, *querida*.' He broke off and

then added roughly, 'I know you don't want to hear this right now, but I still want to be part of your life.'

Olivia closed her eyes for a moment and then opened them again to find his gaze still on her. 'Oh, Christian—' she began, fairly sure she couldn't cope with this in her present state of mind.

But he wouldn't let her finish. 'No,' he interrupted, grasping her hand again. 'Hear me out, *querida*, I beg you. You're alive. That's all that matters. I don't think I could have gone on if—if anything had happened to you.'

'Christian—'

His words were too emotional, too appealing. It would have been so easy to give in and let him have his way. But he didn't really care about her. He just wanted the right to care for his daughter. She refused to subject her child to the disillusionment Luis had had to suffer at his father's hands.

'I'm sorry,' she said at last, wincing as his grip automatically tightened. For a moment, Luis's words came back to her, but she couldn't let anything persuade her from her course. 'I—I appreciate your concern—I do truly—but I can't change the way I feel.'

Christian's lips twisted. 'You still hate me.'

Olivia sighed. 'I never hated you, Christian.'

'But you can never forgive me for what happened, whatever you say.'

'That's not true. I told you weeks ago, we were both to blame for what happened.' She took a trembling breath. 'Now, why don't you be honest and tell me the real reason why you came?'

Christian frowned. 'The real reason?' For a moment he looked blank, but then his face cleared. 'Oh, yes.' He released her wrist and got to his feet. 'I am very sorry that you lost the baby,' he declared formally. 'But it was par for the course, isn't that what they say? Everything that could go wrong has gone wrong, has it not?' He didn't notice her stunned expression but ploughed on wearily, 'But this was never about the baby, *querida*. I think we both know that.'

Olivia could only stare at him disbelievingly, and at last he seemed to notice that something was amiss. 'What is it?' he asked anxiously, resting his hands on the edge of the bed and bending over her. '*Por Dios*, I didn't mean to upset you, Olivia. *Soy idiota*, I'm an idiot. Of course talking about it would upset you, naturally. You are so pale, *querida*. Take it easy. I will go and find a nurse—'

'No!' Somehow she got the word through her strangled vocal cords and put out a hand to stop him. He captured it in both of his, but he still looked apprehensively towards the door. 'What did you say— about the baby?' she asked him hoarsely. 'Please, it's important. Who told you that the baby was dead?'

'Oh, *caramba*, you didn't know,' he exclaimed, his face paling significantly. '*Dios*, what can I say? I thought you knew—'

Olivia squeezed his fingers to stop him. 'Who told you?' she demanded, and he groaned and sank down onto the side of her bed as if he could no longer support himself.

'Luis,' he said wearily. 'He said it was a pity about the baby. Like I said before, he said it was touch and go whether you'd survive.'

Olivia's own eyes were damp now as she realised he'd misunderstood her stepson. She didn't think Luis had deliberately deceived him, but she guessed their conversation hadn't been the friendliest they'd had.

And Luis was sure to have been angry when he'd discovered that Christian was the baby's father. He'd been angry with her and that had never happened before.

Gripping Christian's hand tightly, she said softly, 'The baby's not dead. You have a daughter. I don't know how Luis explained it, but, honestly, she's all right. And if I look shocked it's because you've come here believing I'd lost the baby. I thought it was the baby you cared about, not me.'

Christian looked dazed. 'The baby's alive?' he said blankly, and she nodded.

'Yes.'

'She's all right?'

'She's beautiful. You can see for yourself.' She paused. 'If you like, I'll ring the bell for the nurse and she'll take you to see her.'

'Wait.' Christian's hand gripping hers again stopped her. 'What did you mean about being shocked because I'd come to see you and not the child?' He shook his head. 'Don't you know I was hoping that for once in your life you might need me? That you might let me start again and prove that my feelings are for you, nothing else?'

Olivia trembled. 'Do you mean that?'

Christian grimaced. 'Well, you've heard it before, *querida*. I don't know what else I can say.'

Olivia pressed her lips together for a moment, looking up at him tremulously. 'Just keep on saying it,' she whispered unsteadily. 'Luis might just have done me the biggest favour in the world.'

Christian frowned then, but when Olivia's soft hand cupped his cheek he swiftly turned his mouth into her palm. 'Will you believe me now if I tell you that I love you?' he asked her huskily. '*Dios, querida*, I will always love our daughter because she brought us together. But I will never love anyone as much as I love you…'

EPILOGUE

CHRISTIAN swung his car through the gates that led up to the house he had bought in Boca Raton. The gates closed automatically behind him and he accelerated up the long gravel drive. The house came into view, an attractive sprawling construction, with plenty of room for his growing family.

It was over a year since Olivia had given birth to their daughter, Emilie, and just three weeks since his son, Sebastian, was born. He still felt a quickening of his pulse at the memory of how anxious he'd been when Olivia had told him she was pregnant again. He'd been so afraid they wouldn't be so lucky this time.

But Olivia had remained calm throughout and her second child had presented his mother with no problems at all. Unlike Emilie, who was proving to be quite a handful, Sebastian had arrived with the least amount of fuss.

Susannah now had charge of Emilie, and it was obvious that their erstwhile housekeeper adored both children. Christian had been happy to agree when Olivia had suggested offering her the chance to come with them to Florida. While she'd been recovering from Emilie's birth at the villa on San Gimeno, she and Susannah had become very close.

Of course, he knew the West Indian woman had never forgiven herself for leaving Olivia alone that evening when she'd had to make her own way to the hospital. She should have been with her, she'd said, when she'd arrived at the hospital with tears pouring down her face. Christian's own reaction, when he'd heard the story, had been thank God he'd hired the Jeep in the first place. And it wasn't as if Susannah had been able to drive.

But past anxieties aside, Christian knew he'd never been happier. He loved his wife so much and he knew she felt the same about him. These past thirteen months had proved beyond a shadow of doubt that they'd been meant for each other. And even Luis had had to concede that Olivia deserved her obvious happiness.

For himself, Christian had cut down on his workload, and for the first time since he'd come to work for Tony he was anticipating the day when Luis would be old enough to take command of the Mora Corporation. He still enjoyed his work, of course, but it was no longer the focal point of his existence. His family occupied that place, with Olivia as the centre of his life.

Beyond a flower-strewn veranda, double doors opened into a wide foyer. Here, the atrium-styled ceiling stretched up some fifty feet to a curved glass dome. A crystal chandelier was suspended from a central point and at night cast prisms of light in all directions. But it was late afternoon at present and the sun still cast a golden bloom over the gleaming marble floor.

'Oh, Mr Rodrigues!' A young Filipino maid came to greet him, taking his jacket and briefcase from him and giving him a welcoming smile. 'We didn't expect you home so early. Your wife is still resting. Would you like me to tell her you're here?'

'I'll do that,' said Christian firmly, heading for the curving staircase and taking the treads two at a time. 'Where's Susannah? You can tell her I'm back instead.'

'She's in the garden with Miss Emilie,' replied the maid as he reached the first landing. 'Shall I tell her you want to see her and the little girl?'

'Not right now,' said Christian drily, anticipating a few moments alone with his wife with real pleasure. 'I may just take a shower. It's pretty hot today.'

'Yes, sir.'

The maid accepted her dismissal, and Christian vaulted up the remaining stairs and strode along the first-floor gallery to his suite of rooms. *Dios*, he thought, as he had done so many times before, he must be the luckiest man on earth.

He opened the door to the suite with some caution. If Olivia was resting, then it wouldn't be fair to disturb her. But when he reached the door into their bedroom, he paused ruefully. Olivia was already awake, sitting in the armchair beside the bed, with Sebastian sucking hungrily on her breast.

'Hey,' he said softly, and she glanced across the room in surprise.

'Hey, yourself,' she answered in a low voice, her ready smile embracing him. 'What are you doing home so early?'

'Perhaps I was hoping to do what our son is doing,' he responded drily, treading lightly across the room and bending to kiss his wife. His eyes darkened instinctively as her mouth opened for him, and it was with an effort that he straightened up and dropped down on the bed.

'He's almost finished,' said Olivia comfortingly,

glancing down at Sebastian. 'But he's a hungry little devil. This is his fourth feed today.'

'So long as he isn't tiring you out,' remarked her husband, leaning forward and allowing Sebastian's small fingers to close about one of his. Then he looked at Olivia. 'I want you to myself.'

Olivia's lips twitched. 'Are you jealous?'

'Of this little man?' Christian's smile was rueful. 'Yeah, why not? I'm as jealous as hell.'

'You don't have to be, you know,' Olivia murmured, stretching her free hand out towards him, shivering in delight when he bestowed a moist kiss in her palm.

'I believe you,' he said then, getting up from the bed and pulling his tie free from his collar. 'You know, I think I'll take a shower while you're finishing up here. It's as hot as Hades outside.'

'Take your time,' said Olivia, and Christian headed for the bathroom, shedding his shirt and shoes on the way. He grinned at her before closing the door on her rueful expression. The anticipation could wait until she was free. In fact, it only added to the excitement, but he could use a cooling shower to thin his blood.

Just for a moment, he allowed his mind to drift back to the night he'd got that anonymous phone call. He never had found out who the caller was. But, significantly, he'd learned that that was the moment Emilie had been born, and he chose to think that Olivia's need had reached out to him.

He was still standing there, allowing the spray to pour down on him, when the door of the cubicle opened and Olivia slipped in with him. 'Let me,' she said, reaching round him for the soap, and he felt her soft breasts against his back. She began by lathering his waist and buttocks, but Christian found that cold water could only achieve so much.

'*Dios,*' he groaned, when her hands slid round his waist and began to soap his stomach. His manhood, already aching with need, sprang instantly to attention at the brush of her hands. Twisting round, he took the soap and returned the favour, soaping her arms and shoulders. Then bent his head and took one milk-scented nipple into his mouth.

Her moan of pleasure was almost too much for him, but when she would have taken his hand to pull him out of the cubicle, he held her back.

'What's wrong with right here?' he asked, cupping her buttocks in his hands and lifting her against the glass panels. Then, with the utmost care, he allowed her to slide down onto him and she instantly convulsed around his shaft.

'God, Christian,' she whispered, 'that was incredible.'

'We aim to please,' he mouthed against her lobe, his tongue finding the pulse that raced beneath her ear. 'Are you all right? I'm not hurting you?'

'Not at all,' she said shakily, tilting her head back to give him total access. 'Oh, yes, Christian, please. Do that again.'

An hour later they were recovering in the cool luxury of their four-poster. The huge bed had been transported from an antebellum mansion that had been falling into disrepair. With Christian's help, the mansion had been rescued for posterity, and the bed had been expertly renovated and presented to him as a gift.

'Sleepy?' Christian asked, tucking a damp strand of her hair behind her ear, and Olivia stretched voluptuously.

'Contented,' she corrected him gently. 'You must come home early every day. This has been fun.'

'You won't say that when you want to get on with your new story about Dimdum,' Christian reminded her. Her first story had eventually been accepted by its fourth would-be publisher and was presently having a moderate success.

'Oh, I'm in no hurry to continue Dimdum's adventures,' Olivia admitted. 'Now that I've got children of my own, I can tell my stories to them. Perhaps when they're older, when you're getting bored with me, I'll do something to make you proud of me again.'

'I'll never be bored with you,' Christian assured her fiercely. '*Dios, querida,* when I think how close I came to losing you, I want to throw up. I love you. I'll always love you. Never, ever, doubt that. You're everything I've ever wanted. You're my wife, the mother of my children, and—simply, my life.'

The world's bestselling romance series.

Seduction and Passion Guaranteed!

Mama Mia!

They're tall, dark...and ready to marry!

Don't delay, pick up the next story in
this great new miniseries...pronto!

On sale this month
MARCO'S PRIDE by Jane Porter #2385

Coming in April
HIS INHERITED BRIDE by Jacqueline Baird #2385

Don't miss
May 2004
THE SICILIAN HUSBAND by Kate Walker #2393

July 2004
THE ITALIAN'S DEMAND by Sara Wood #2405

Pick up a Harlequin Presents® novel and you will
enter a world of spine-tingling passion and
provocative, tantalizing romance!

Available wherever Harlequin books are sold.

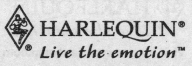

Live the emotion™

Visit us at www.eHarlequin.com

HPITHUSB

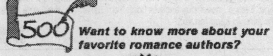

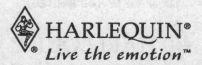

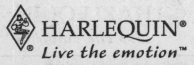

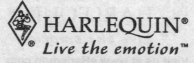

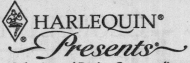

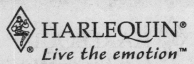